Sorrow
&
Bliss

Kalyn Hazel

CHAPTER 1: AZURE

"Basel, I'm dying."

"Uh huh, Azure," Basel mumbles back distractedly, more focused on the reports spread out in front of him than whatever nonsense Azure is talking about today.

"No, seriously. I'm dying. I can feel that the end is near," Azure trails off dramatically.

"Azure, shut the hell up. I need to finish these."

Azure flips over onto his stomach on the bed to look up at Basel next to him, "I'm dying and you don't even care."

Basel huffs impatiently and turns to face him with feigned patience. "Okay, let's pretend for a moment that you're not full of shit and that you're actually dying, why?"

"Because my other half isn't here," Azure answers simply.

Basel looks at him in confusion. "Your other half? Who?" He rolls his eyes as realization hits him. "Ocher? Really Azure? You interrupted me for that?"

"I'm kidding, I'm kidding." He laughs. "I really am dying though. I think I manipulated too much energy and it's slowly killing me."

Now Basel looks concerned. "What? I mean, I shouldn't be surprised because I'm still kind of shocked that you can do what you do, but there's side effects?"

"Yeah," he sighs. "The amplifier I ate makes me stronger, but it takes way more of my energy than I can replenish. I've been feeling myself getting weaker for a while, now it's actually getting bad."

"Shouldn't you have considered the side effects *before* you nearly burned a city to the ground?"

"Well, I didn't care what happened to me before. It didn't matter if it killed me because I wasn't expecting to live too much longer anyway."

"But you care now," Basel guesses.

"Unfortunately."

"Because of your *other half.*"

"Obviously."

"Your other half who isn't even here with you. Who you haven't seen in close to a year."

Azure flops over onto his back and shuts his eyes against Basel's skeptical look. "Minor disagreement."

"Uh huh," he answers, dragging the words out slowly enough that Azure can tell Basel doesn't believe him.

"Shouldn't you be advising something?"

"I could advise you to shut up and not interrupt me," Basel offers.

"You're the worst excuse for an advisor. In fact, you're the perfect example of why people should be chosen based on merits and not their connections."

"A little late for that. Please show yourself out of my room."

"It's a guest room," Azure corrects him. "You don't get a room here. This is my home."

"I stay here when I'm forced to come advise, so it's my room. Get out before I call the guards."

"The guards are terrified of me," Azure laughs.

Basel doesn't respond, once again absorbed in his reports and Azure lets him be. There's a limit to Basel's patience and he never gives him as much attention as Ocher did anyway. Although, at least he's here. Ocher's gone and hasn't been heard from since, so much for his worthless promises. It would serve Ocher right if he came back and found him dead.

Speaking of which, he really doesn't know how much time he has left. There's no information about consequences and he's definitely not interested in going back to Meio to beg them for answers. Well, more like threaten them because even with begging, they probably wouldn't be willing to tell him anything.

On the bright side, at least he was able to live his last days in luxury as the leader of Haithen. Not many people can say that. When he's on his deathbed, he could have people feeding and doting on him 24/7 until he died. Even though it would suck to die while he's still young and beautiful with what could have been years ahead of him.

"Okay Azure," Basel says as he gathers the reports into a neat stack. "I'm assuming you're here in my room because you're lonely. You claim this is about you dying and maybe it is, but you wanted some company too."

"So what if I did? I'm allowed to talk to other people."

"No one said you weren't and since it doesn't look like Ocher will be back anytime soon, let's put that aside. What are you going to do about your inevitable death?"

"We all die eventually."

"Azure."

He exhales quietly, "There's nothing I *can* do. I don't know if there's a way to reverse the damage and no one to ask."

"You can't ask those water people?"

"I won't. Besides, they wouldn't tell me anyway."

"So, you're just going to let it happen and die?"

"Yeah," he shrugs. "Two years late."

Basel shakes his head, "And what about Haithen?"

"I don't care what happens to Haithen. I'll be dead, remember? They can kill each other trying to take control and it won't matter to me."

"Well...I guess this is goodbye. What kind of flowers do you want at your funeral?"

"Orange Blossoms. And I want my body taken back to my village and buried there. Then, I want the whole place turned into a memorial. Kick out those squatters that live there now."

Basel stares at him for a moment, "You've thought about this."

"Of course. I've known for a while." Basel opens his mouth when a knock on the door interrupts him. "Come in!" Azure shouts.

"This is *my* room."

"My home."

"Not for long," Basel mutters.

One of his staff members opens the door looking apologetic. "I apologize for the interruption, but a meeting is about to be held and your presence is needed."

Azure sits up and swings his legs over the bed, "How did you know I was here?"

"We didn't. Someone else was sent to get you. His presence as an advisor was required as well."

"Oh. Come on then. Maybe it's something exciting."

"It's never anything exciting," Basel replies, falling into step next to him as they're led to the meeting hall.

They're the last two to arrive and every chair is filled except the three at the head of the table, reserved for him, his second, and that traitor who would occasionally come to meetings when he had nothing else to do. It's been a year, he should have that chair removed, or torched.

Azure drops into his seat, "Let's hear it. What urgently boring business has come up now?"

"You are aware of the situation with all the refugees from the east, correct?" His second adviser, Kronos, asks him.

"Of course. They're very nice, helpful people."

Kronos' mouth turns down slightly, but he doesn't counter with his own less polite opinion. "Well, it's been two years since you've taken over and under your new rule, there has been an increase in the number of refugees traveling throughout our country. They no longer feel a need to hide."

"And what's wrong with that? We're not taking any more third children or forcing people to live in fear of being arrested for treason."

"This is true," Kronos concedes. "*However,* they still show no interest in assimilating into our general population, instead they continue to live in their caravans and drive them across the country, even more mobile now than before. We have received complaints from the citizens. They want it stopped."

"They never would have complained before."

"That's because they had bigger worries that *you* have now taken care of," Basel comments.

"Give them an inch and they want a mile. And what would you have me do? Throw them all out?"

"Not quite. We think it would be more beneficial if they returned to their own homeland willingly."

Azure stares at the faces around the table blankly, "If they wanted to go home, this wouldn't be an issue. They're *refugees.*"

"Let me be blunt," a third adviser interrupts. "You have given autonomy back to most of the countries that border us to the east and they also do not want the refugees interfering with the reestablishment of their countries and people. The refugees come from Vita, which is farther east. We need you, as the new leader, to make an official visit to Vita and assess the situation."

"And do what?" Azure exclaims. "See if it's too miserable to force them back to?" This is ridiculous, who cares if the citizens don't like it, they should just be happy they have their freedoms back.

"No. We want you to visit Vita, assess the situation, and determine what can be done. If it's not as bad as they say, simply encourage their government to do something about the emigration of their people and if it is as bad as they pretend, then a hostile takeover may be necessary. We can make plans to take out the leaders, set up a new government, and then encourage the refugees to return home."

"Do you all live to fight? Are your lives not fulfilling enough without someone to control?" The population of their army has been reduced because they're no longer enforcing Haithen's laws on the other countries. People live in peace and these advisers want him to start another war? It makes no sense to him.

"Of course not. You could attempt to negotiate with them first and work with them, then a hostile takeover wouldn't even be necessary. Everyone should have a safe home that they can return to."

Azure opens his mouth to question where that concern was the past few years when they sat idly by and let people be killed, but Kronos has taken over again before he gets the chance. "Either way, we don't know much about Vita and it's important to know our neighbors. Our expansion never made it that far and they are an unknown entity to us. For all we know, they could be preparing to attack *us*. No matter what decision you make on how to resolve the situation, it would only benefit us to know more about the country and if we're not going to war, then to have a good relationship with them."

"Are we done here?" Azure questions.

"That is our most pressing concern, yes."

"Fine." He gets up and leaves, musing over their words as Basel follows behind him. Once again, he really doesn't care what happens to Haithen once he's gone and what are the chances that Vita is planning an attack against them when they've done nothing all these years?

They would also know about it far in advance because Vita would have to go through one of the countries to Haithen's east first. Maybe the caravans aren't great for the land, but he's not interested in forcing all the refugees out. They helped him and that makes them even. So what if they don't want to assimilate? Haithen doesn't exactly have the best reputation. Who would want to be part of this country?

"You don't agree with them?" Basel asks.

"I don't. And I also don't see why they can't go themselves since they're so much better at making plans and connections than I am. I don't believe for a second that they picked me because I'm the leader."

"No, I think that's exactly why they picked you." Basel holds up a hand against his protests, "Let me explain. Vita is an unknown. They have no idea what to expect if we go there. If it's not that bad, they can get rid of the refugees and if it's terrible, maybe they can get rid of you. It's unknown, you might get killed over there and they're probably hoping for it. In either case, they gain a win."

"Ah, so as the leader, I'm the most expendable person to them."

Basel nods, "Absolutely. They want you gone the most. Then they'll probably share power between themselves."

"And what about you?"

"When I see that coming, I'm quitting while I'm ahead."

"And running back to your tower?"

"Of course. Which will happen whether you go over there and get killed or die here, whichever happens first."

"Positive, aren't you?"

Basel shrugs, "You're the one who said you were dying."

Azure contemplates what undertaking another journey would cost him. He was telling the truth when he told Basel that he didn't know how much longer he had left and this might be something interesting to do considering he hasn't gone far in almost a year.

He doubts there's anything too dangerous to the east, so he can get there and back quick enough in case he takes a turn for the worse. Most importantly though, this could be an excuse to seek out Ocher. He can at least wrap up those loose ends before he dies, but he'll wait to determine if that's a good or bad thing. For all he knows Ocher could be living his best life now and may not want him back in it. There's only one way to find out and if Ocher doesn't want anything to do with him, at least he won't have to live with that knowledge for long.

"What's that look on your face? Did you make up your mind?"

"Yes," he turns to Basel with a smile, already knowing the other male won't approve. "I think I'll find Ocher and go check it out."

Basel stares at him for a moment, conflicting emotions flashing in his hazel eyes. "And where is Ocher, Azure?" He finally asks.

"Somewhere. It shouldn't be too hard to track him down."

"Maybe he won't want to go with you."

"It's Ocher we're talking about," he says as they head back to his rooms.

"Yeah and he's been gone a year. A lot can change in that time,"

Basel counters.

"I know him better than you." Well used to, Azure thinks. He had never expected Ocher to run off and actually stay gone without a word for so long. A month at most was what he had thought, but it became more and more apparent that Ocher wasn't planning on coming back as the months passed. The asshole. Broke all his promises and left.

"It'd be a shame if you find out that you don't know him as well as you think. Call me when you find him and I'll come join you."

"Don't you have things to do here?"

"Just as many as you. I could use a break too."

Azure scoffs, Basel barely works. He sits around letting everyone else make the decisions while he absorbs everything they say and gets his paycheck. Still, it wouldn't be too bad if Basel came along. There would be at least one person on his side.

CHAPTER 2: OCHER

Ocher wakes up at the crack of dawn, a habit he still hasn't broken despite all the mornings Azure would keep him in bed until after sunrise. He still dreams of the familiar weight of an arm over his waist, fingers curled into his own. It's been almost a year, but he still aches for Azure and it's been worse the past few days. No longer just an emotional feeling, now the burning in his heart is a physical sensation.

It doesn't matter, he doesn't even know how to go back at this point. What would Azure say? Would he even take him back or has he already moved on? And the most vital question, would anything between them change or would Azure still control everything? It's one of the reasons he left, to experience the world for himself away from Azure's influence.

It's not that he regrets leaving because he doesn't. He's learned so much on his own about how the world works and how to survive in it. It's only when he's alone that he misses the familiarity of Azure's presence.

One day he'll get over that too. That's not his life anymore, he's built something new outside of Azure's whims. He has his own friends, his own life, just for him. All his choices are his own now.

He crawls out of bed after another restless night and climbs down the ladder from his loft. His room is small. It consists of his lofted bed, a couch on the floor beneath it, and a few possessions with just enough floor space for a few people to stand in, if they're wedged in tight.

His home for the past year isn't much, but it's all he needs for himself.

It's still gray with just a hint of pink peeking over the horizon when he steps outside. He can read well enough now, but outside of his life with Azure, Ocher had very quickly realized the only skills he possessed were physical. And since he didn't want to kill for money, physical labor was his best option.

He ended up in an out of the way town whose main source of survival were the various farms surrounding it. Almost everyone in the town worked on one in some form or another, so it was easy enough to get a job here.

The work isn't hard, there's plenty of food, and he assumes it pays well, although he doesn't know for sure because he's not good with money, Azure had always taken care of that.

The first half of his day is spent outside managing the fifty rows of crops he's responsible for and once the day turns hotter, the second half is spent inside processing his assigned harvest. Everything is straightforward and there are no hurdles to jump through or captains on power trips watching. It's perfect for him.

The only problem that causes him any stress is...the twins, Erina and Eren. He's been able to deflect them this long and they don't push, but sometimes he can tell they want more from him than he's willing to give.

He's not ready. Azure still has too much of a hold on him, getting involved with anyone else right now is more than he can handle. Even if they're kind and give him space.

"Ocher," a pale hand rests on his shoulders and he flinches. "I didn't mean to surprise you. Are you eating breakfast with us?" He looks up to see Erina standing beside him and gives her an apologetic smile. Her brown hair is tightly plaited into a french braid and she looks at him with fond exasperation in her deep brown eyes. "You really don't have to work half as hard as you do, no one else does."

Ocher shrugs, "It's fine. I don't mind it. It gives me something to do."

"That's not how most people think of work, but with how you were raised, I guess you're used to it by now." She leads him to the blanket where Eren is already spreading out food and takes a seat. "It's fine to relax once in a while."

Eren looks up at their arrival and sends him another blinding smile that he never knows how to respond to. "Yeah, Ocher, have a little fun sometimes!" Eren pulls him by the hand to sit between them in the only open spot and he knows it's intentional. The two of them seem to have come to a compromise and agreed to share him for now.

He's still not sure how he feels about that, but their subtle fighting over him used to be much worse. At least this way he doesn't have to pretend to ignore it. He's made it clear that he's not interested in going that way with either of them, but they took it more as his insecurity and inexperience rather than disinterest and he has a feeling they're both still waiting for him to pick one of them.

That's never going to happen if he has anything to say about it. He'd run away first. So long as they continue to consider him an orphan too shy to move further, he can be left to himself. He doesn't want the weight of anyone else's emotions on him, it's draining and he can barely deal with his own emotions.

A plate is forced into his hands, but not before Eren steals a piece of fruit off with a bright grin. Ocher gives him a half smile, debating on whether to just dump the whole plate and wait until he's done working to eat. The only reason he doesn't is because they brought it to him and despite everything, they've been welcoming since he arrived here. The transition to independence would have been much harder without their easy acceptance of him. He's not going to throw that back in their faces.

Erina's hand on his arm draws his attention from Eren's grin to her concerned gaze and he fights not to shake her hand off. "Are you okay? You seem distant today."

"I'm still not sleeping well. It's been worse lately, the pain makes it hard to sleep at night."

"You really should see a doctor, you know. We have two here."

"I know, but it's really not that important."

She gives him a dubious look, "A few days ago you almost fell asleep against one of the machines. That's dangerous."

That was a one time thing, Ocher thinks. The pain in his heart had just started up and he'd slept badly combined with a loss of appetite, so he'd skipped breakfast. He'd almost passed out and had been sent home for the day, but it hadn't solved anything.

"Why don't you go take a nap after breakfast?" Eren suggests. "You always start so early that you finish before everyone anyway. Take a nap, you can finish the day out with us, and then we can have dinner together."

Everything except the last part of that suggestion sounds good, but he agrees anyway. The pain in his chest lessens during the day, so maybe it will last long enough for him to get some rest. "I'll do that."

Eren beams at him and he returns the look with a small smile before dropping his gaze. He's learned that the longer he looks, the more of a wrong impression they get. Handling people is exhausting.

After eating, he heads back to his small room in the communal building and climbs into his loft. Even with the curtains drawn, it's bright inside and Ocher sighs, he can't sleep like this. Azure prefers complete darkness, so by proxy he still does too.

He turns over and catches sight of his bare wrist, the skin there has long since darkened to match the rest of his arm. Ocher touches his wrist lightly. It's not like he needs anything else to remind him of Azure, but sometimes he still can't believe he lost it.

Azure has been feeding him his favorite food, chilled raspberries, for the past thirty minutes. They're even topped with whipped cream. That's not a cause for suspicion because Azure does occasionally get into a mood where he feels overly affectionate for a while. What is suspicious is the fact that he's doting without saying a word for this long.

Something rude usually follows by now and that hasn't happened yet. Instead he's wrapped in Azure's arms, waiting for the other shoe to drop, and even he has a limit to how many raspberries he can eat.

He pushes Azure's arm away the next time a raspberry comes near his mouth and looks up at him, "What's going on?"

"What do you mean?"

"This. It's not like you."

"I can't be nice?"

Ocher pushes himself upright, "You're never nice like this."

"Just because you take my niceness for granted doesn't mean I'm not. You get it the most and besides, why shouldn't I be nice to you? You're mine."

He rolls his eyes, "You seem to like rubbing that in my face."

"It's true," Azure answers. "And you never deny it."

Like he's going to deny it and deal with Azure's petulance until he eventually caves and agrees with him. Besides, it's mostly true anyway. "What do you want, Azure?"

Azure sighs and pulls a small box out of his pocket that he throws hard enough to hurt when it hits him in the chest. "Some people don't know how to enjoy a good thing."

"With you, I've learned to ask questions when you act differently," Ocher replies, opening the box. Inside is an obsidian bangle, shining in the light. Each end is capped with a deep sapphire gem. Ocher pulls it out, letting it rest heavily in his hand. On the inside, there's a delicate pattern of fire traced in gold.

Ocher looks between the no doubt expensive item in his hand and Azure's feigned air of indifference. He wouldn't do this on a whim. The fact that it took Azure so long to work up to giving it to him says that this means more to Azure than he wants to let on.

Azure does spoil him, but this is on another level. This is sincere. Sincere enough that he probably spent weeks deciding if he wanted to open himself up this much. Azure's actions are always much more honest than his words.

"You love me."

The words slip out before he can stop them, but he knows they're true. That's the only reason Azure would do this. It's been almost a year and most of the time, it's hard to know how Azure really feels about him. If there's actual affection or if he's kept around because he almost always gives into Azure's wants. This leaves no doubt. He might not have Azure's full trust at times, but willingly or not, he has his heart.

Azure's eyes widen slightly and he falls back onto the bed, breaking eye contact. "I would never say that."

"You don't have to." Ocher slides the bangle around his wrist and climbs over Azure to cage him in with his arms and legs, watching how Azure's gaze hovers over the wrist where his new gift sits. "I guess there's more than one reason you keep me around."

Azure finally turns his head to look up at him with heated cobalt eyes, "There's several reasons I keep you around."

Ocher is pulled from sleep gradually, unsure if he's still dreaming or not. Someone's hand is under his shirt, letting their fingers draw shapes against his stomach. It could be one of the twins, though he can't imagine either of them being bold enough to climb into his bed and touch him like this.

He shifts and the fingers on his stomach still. There's no point pretending he's asleep now. Ocher opens his eyes and his breath catches. Azure is beside him, watching him with deep blue eyes. Ocher blinks a couple of times in confusion because how is this possible? How did Azure locate him and find out where he lives? Even when he pulls back a bit, Azure is still there, same eyes and same familiar mouth laughing quietly at him. He remembers how that laughter felt against his lips.

Azure breaks the silence between them and leans forward to give him a chaste kiss, "Hey love."

"I don't...what are you doing here?" He can't wrap his head around Azure being here, in his *bed* with no warning. Did no one try to stop a strange guy from breaking into his room?

"I came to see you obviously. Did you miss me?"

Ocher glances over at Azure, still as unreadable as ever, and *yes* he missed him. He missed almost everything about him. For as much as Azure could be a bully, he was notoriously good at catering to him when he wanted to.

"No," Ocher lies. He won't show weakness until he finds out what Azure really wants.

Azure sits up with a laugh. "Sure, you didn't. That's why you can't decide if you want to push me away or not." He presses a hand against Ocher's thighs, "Open."

What? "Azure, I don't think we should be doing this."

"Oh? So you admit *we* are doing this."

"That's not what I said," Ocher protests, but Azure is already pushing his legs apart to settle between them and stupidly, he barely even resists.

Azure's hands come to rest on the waistband on his pants.

"Haven't been in this position in oh say *a year?*" He freezes, not wanting to let this go any further. There's something in Azure's tone that says he hasn't been forgiven for leaving.

"Azure, wait." Ocher grabs hold of his hands before Azure can get his pants down past his knees. He's always been terrible at denying Azure and it seems like a year apart hasn't changed that.

"Isn't a year long enough to wait?"

"Yeah, I mean no! Azure!" He squirms as Azure gets a hand around him, squeezing tighter when Ocher pushes at his arm. "Azure, listen, this isn't a good idea."

Dark blue eyes study his face, "Why isn't it?" His hand makes a few quick movements and Ocher bites back a quiet noise. Azure watches him curiously, "How long has it been since you were last touched this way, Ocher? You're very responsive."

Like hell he's going to answer that. He knows Azure, no matter what his answer is, he's going to get a reaction that's bad for him.

Azure's free hand is tugging at his underwear when the door opens and the twins enter. If he wasn't so embarrassed, he'd be relieved. They stare up at them with twin looks of surprise. He can't blame them, he's made it a point to avoid even hinting at what he might like.

"Someone said they saw someone new heading in here," Erina begins. "But, I guess…you're okay with that."

Ocher can't help thinking how terrible this looks. He's made it clear to the two of them that he doesn't want any kind of relationship, yet here he is with a complete stranger to them and his pants around his knees. The only bright point is that their interruption kept him from doing something he might come to regret.

He covers his face with his hands to block out Azure's smug smile and the twin's betrayed gazes. They've been good to him since he arrived here, helping him whenever he needed. "I'm sorry."

"We'll just...leave you alone," he hears Eren mumble before the door shuts.

The second they leave, Azure is yanking his hands away from his face, "What are you apologizing for?" He demands to know. "Did you tell them I was your ex and you were through with me?"

"You're not my ex. We never dated."

"Look at you, so informed now." Azure taunts.

Ocher swats Azure's hands away from him, but there's no heat behind it. Instead he brings his hands to Azure's neck to pull lightly and Azure leans down obediently.

Azure stares into his eyes, close enough that the long strands of his hair brush against his face. It's been so long since Azure has looked at him like this, like he's everything. "Hey...I missed you," Azure tells him, voicing Ocher's own thoughts.

"I bet you did," Ocher responds instead of matching his confession. He pulls Azure down into a kiss and he comes eagerly, already sliding hands down his thighs in anticipation, but Ocher doesn't give him the chance to go further.

He manages to get his leg between them and kicks Azure off him before hastily yanking up his pants and escaping down the ladder.

Azure props up on one arm to look down at him in mild annoyance. "That was rude."

"No worse than you sneaking into my room when I was asleep," Ocher counters.

"Don't act like you didn't used to do that all the time with me."

"It's different," he insists, even though Azure has a point. There were many times Azure was asleep and he came crawling into his bed. He was *always* welcomed.

"Where are you going? Tell me not to them. You don't owe them anything."

"They're my friends."

"Then I guess you can go apologize since you're not available. You might be breaking their hearts, but at least you won't destroy their sibling bond."

Ocher freezes with his hand on the doorknob. How could Azure know that? How could he know how they feel about him or even that they're siblings? In fact, how did Azure know the perfect time to catch him alone?

He turns back to meet Azure's mischievous gaze, "How long have you been here?"

"A few days. Just observing the new life you decided to create."

"You're the worst."

"It's not my fault that you didn't know I was here. Previously you would have been able to feel it."

Then, it all makes sense. He *did* feel it. The burning pain in his heart that had been keeping him up. The pain probably started the exact moment Azure came back into close proximity to him and the possibility hadn't even occurred to him.

"*Did* you feel it?"

"I should have known it was you. Who else would announce themselves by causing me pain instead of just talking to me?" He replies instead of answering the question.

"Maybe I had to decide if you were worth talking to first."

"I can't say I'm glad you found me worthy," he mutters, swinging the door open and letting it shut on Azure. Ten minutes and Azure is already under his skin.

Ocher finds Erina and Eren inside one of the mess halls, eating together quietly. They were probably coming to invite him to lunch when they walked in on that scene, and the thought makes him feel that much guiltier.

"Um...hi," he begins awkwardly, trailing off when they look at him with varying degrees of betrayal. He tries again. "I'm sorry about that."

"Who was he?" Eren questions impatiently.

"He was my friend." Is Azure his friend? No, but it's the easiest explanation. They never put a name to their relationship or even discussed it besides Azure demanding to be his one and only.

"He looked like more than a friend," Erina says.

Ocher sighs, "I didn't know he was here."

"But you let him..." Eren gestures helplessly, unable to finish the sentence.

"Yeah, I shouldn't have. He surprised me."

"Were you two -" Eren stops abruptly, eyes flicking over his shoulder and Ocher already knows what he'll see.

"I'll be right back," he excuses himself and pushes Azure back out the doors before he has a chance to start goading the twins. "What are you doing here?"

"I already told you why I'm here."

"No! Azure, why are you here? Tell me the truth."

"Always so wrapped up in *truth*. It never did you any favors. Haithen wants to know more about our neighbors to the far east and why so many people leave there. As the current ruler, I *magnanimously* volunteered to go take a look, even though we don't control anywhere else anymore. The other countries are still recovering and building back up, so it's the least we could do for those that are getting an influx of guests." He smiles. "And I thought, who better to go with me than my old traveling buddy?" Azure drapes an arm around his shoulders and pulls him in closer.

"Traveling buddy."

"What would you call yourself?" Ocher looks away, he's not going to be the one to put a name to them, especially with the distance he can feel between them now. "That's what I thought. Are you coming with me or not?"

He's reluctant, but at the same time he wonders, is this the way back? He's missed Azure and although he doubts slipping back into each other's lives will be easy, this could be his only opportunity to repair how broken he left them or to find out where they stand, for better or worse. If he says no, Azure may never seek him out again and if he's ever ready to return, he might be refused.

"Okay."

"When will you be ready to go?"

"You're leaving, Ocher?" Erina's surprised voice questions from behind them.

Ocher turns to face her and Eren, "Just for a little while."

"Maybe," Azure adds and Ocher nudges him quiet.

"He wants me to go somewhere with him. I'm not sure for how long."

Eren points towards the edge of town where Ocher can just make out something large and black. "Did he drive that giant vehicle here?"

"Yep, that's mine," Azure answers. "The place is a little far."

"It's big."

"I know."

"Then you have room for one more," Eren points out, holding his gaze.

"No, two more," Erina corrects.

"I don't think - " Ocher begins before being cut off with a tight squeeze around his shoulders.

"Sounds like a great idea!" Azure agrees. "The more, the merrier."

"Azure..." Ocher looks at him in suspicion. What is he playing at? He's sure Azure doesn't care about these two at all and he's *always* worse when there are other people around. He, himself, doesn't even want them to come. It's taken a year to build up his persona, it would unravel so fast with Azure in the picture. Then, this town wouldn't even be the safe place he could return to because everyone would know about the part of himself he keeps hidden.

Fingers run up the back of his neck, trailing under his hair and brushing at the nape of his neck. Instinctively, he leans into the touch, eyelids lowering as the gentle touch relaxes him. "Don't you want your new friends to come with us, Ocher? People bond so well when they travel together, you remember?"

He doesn't bother answering. Azure will do what he wants either way and this feels nice. Ocher can't help the small sound of protest that escapes him when Azure moves his hand away. He looks over and Azure is watching him with a small smirk, and even worse, the twins are looking at him funny.

Ocher steps back out of Azure's reach, hating Azure for knowing him and all his weak spots so well. He had a year to learn them all and Azure made sure he did, completely.

"I've got to do one last thing before we leave," Azure tells him. "So, how about we leave tomorrow morning, does that work?"

"Yeah."

Once Azure leaves them, he should go back to work, instead he turns towards his building. He just can't gather the motivation to work after that. He'd like to go somewhere alone and sift through what just happened, but the way Erina and Eren are looking at him says that won't be possible.

"Ocher, who is he really?" Eren asks, sliding closer into his space.

He takes a step back, "I already told you, he's one of my friends."

"No regular person has a vehicle like that. In fact, citizens *can't* own any that big."

"He works for the government."

"And you trust him enough to go with him?" Erina asks.

"You two don't have to come with me."

"No, we're definitely coming. You might trust him, but we don't."

"You don't even know him."

"Well, *you* don't even seem to like him that much," Eren points out.

"It's not that, we just haven't talked in a while."

"More reason not to trust him."

"Alright," Ocher gives in. He's not going to argue with them and if he did manage to convince them not to come, Azure might invite them again to spite him.

He glances around the small town on the way back to his room to start packing. This might be the last time he ever lives here and he doesn't know if that makes him happy or sad to realize.

This town has been his home for almost a year and leaving it means Azure, but Azure also means the loss of independence. Why is it so hard to have both?

Azure is waiting for them the next morning, near the edge of town in one of the few spots big enough to keep his vehicle without interrupting everyone's daily routine. Now that he's not keeping his appearance a secret, his arrival is on the tip of everyone's tongue. Although no one received any information from him. Once he'd shaken off the twins, he'd locked himself in his room for the rest of the day.

Ocher drops his bag in Azure's unsuspecting lap and the other boy looks up at him blankly. "Are we leaving or not?"

Azure glances behind him to see if the twins are there too and adjusts his bag into a firmer hold. "Not yet, we're waiting for one more person."

"Who?" Nobody else here knows Azure, the gossip yesterday was proof enough of that.

"Someone. If you're so impatient, you can kiss me while we wait."

He wrinkles his nose, "Pass."

"Your loss."

"I've lived for a year without feeling the need."

Azure's eyes narrow and without warning, he launches Ocher's bag back at him, sending him to the ground. "Oh, I'm sorry Ocher. Didn't realize how weak you had become from living out here for so long."

"You're an ass," he breathes out.

"I see some things never change," an amused voice cuts in before Azure can respond and Ocher feels his stomach drop when he looks up to see Basel walking towards them, dragging a suitcase behind him.

"You brought *him! Azure why?*" Ocher winces internally at how whiny he sounds.

Azure laughs and steps around him to greet Basel. "You have your friends, I deserve one too."

"I don't want to go anymore. I'm staying."

"No, you're not. Get in."

Eren and Erina arrive then and reach down to help him up. He nods his thanks and throws all three of their bags in the back before reaching for the passenger door.

"Nope," Azure cuts him off. My friend up front, you and your friends in the back. After all, they like you so much. I wouldn't want to deprive them."

Ocher reluctantly climbs into the backseat and ends up sand-wiched between the two siblings. Azure and Basel are up front, joking back and forth and he hates it, knowing he's going to have to endure this the entire time.

Azure turns around to smile at him, "You still pout as cutely as ever."

"Shut up," Ocher responds.

"I've never seen him pout the entire time we've known him," Erina says, looking at him curiously.

Azure smirks and turns back to the front, "Ocher definitely gets in his moods."

Both twins look at him and Ocher sinks lower in his seat. Al-ready, things are falling apart.

Basel reclines his seat and winks one amused hazel eye back at them, "This is gonna be a trip."

CHAPTER 3: AZURE

There's two additional passengers that he hadn't planned for on this trip. When he first arrived in town and saw how the two of them had attached themselves to Ocher, he was annoyed. When it became clear that Ocher didn't return the feelings of either one of them, his annoyance turned to spiteful amusement.

For a moment he was worried that Ocher really had changed. Two people that cared for him so easily would have been enticing, especially for someone like Ocher who likes to be cared for. The Ocher he knew wouldn't have let himself get attached to anyone the way they used to be, he'd spent a year making sure of it. Even so, there was always that slight fear he would have opened himself up to a different kind of relationship. One that wasn't all-consuming and that allowed for compromise.

He shouldn't have worried.

Ocher doesn't do anything without a little pressure on him and these two don't have the spine for it. So he'd thought, why not let the two of them come along? Ocher clearly didn't want them to, probably because he's been pretending to be someone he's not. All the more reason to have them. He can deal with some extra baggage if it strains Ocher's relationship with the twins, and he knows it will. The way they act with him tells Azure that they barely know him at all and Ocher won't be able to keep that facade up forever.

Their first stop is in a city a few towns over to pick up supplies. He hadn't brought anything except his own bag because he wasn't sure what would actually happen once he found Ocher. Basel could have been right about their relationship for once in his life.

Stares follow after them when he parks in the middle of the street and all five of them exit the vehicle. It's been two years since he took over, but people still remember what military vehicles like his meant and they're rightfully wary.

Azure disregards their looks and enters the store, leaving the others to linger under the stares. He has to purchase enough supplies for four people now and they need tents. Two tents should be enough for them and he drops them in a basket as he searches for anything else they might need. Blankets because he's assuming the temperature will be lower in the mountains. Too bad he's not planning on letting Ocher cuddle up with him.

"You're buying them a tent too?" Basel questions, peering over his shoulder.

"Where else are they supposed to sleep in case we have to camp?"

"Blankets too?" He sifts through the basket, "Why are you spending your money on them? You don't even know them. Make them buy their own supplies since they wanted to come."

"Quit being so cheap, Basel."

"I'm not cheap, I'm *frugal.* They can buy their own tents."

"And if they can't, are you going to share with them?" Azure counters.

"No! In fact, since you're feeling so generous, buy me one too!"

Azure rolls his eyes and hefts another one into his basket. "You're getting just as spoiled as Ocher was."

"Hah!" Basel sidles in closer to him and throws an arm around his shoulders, "Does that mean I get all the same privileges he used to have as well?"

Azure glances at him, "The privilege of living in my mansion? You've already claimed a room there."

"No, the *physical* privileges." Basel gives him a knowing look and Azure shakes his head, pushing the cart forward.

"Um, where exactly are we going?" A feminine voice questions from behind him, so it must be the girl.

"Shouldn't you have asked that before you packed up and left your home?"

"Yes, but we didn't. Making sure Ocher wasn't in trouble was more important."

"He is trouble," Azure mutters. "Why are you all following me?"

"Because you're the only one who knows where we are and where we're going."

"We're going to make some new acquaintances."

"Why do you need Ocher to come?" She pries.

"I didn't, he wanted to come."

"That doesn't make sense. You're with the other guy, why would Ocher want to come along on your trip?"

"I don't know!" Azure exclaims. "He's back there with you two. You're closer to him than I am! Why don't you ask him?" He already has a low tolerance for questions. Questions about his relationship with Ocher cross a hard line.

Someone needs to let them know that he has no problem opening the door and kicking them out in the middle of nowhere. Ocher too, if he objects.

Basel nudges him in the side and drops out of step with him to grab onto the male twin, "Come on you two. You can help get food since you're coming with us." He ignores their protests and hauls both of them back towards the entrance, leaving only Ocher to trail silently behind him through the store.

It hasn't been this awkward between them in years, not since they first met, apparently that's what distance will do after you've thrown someone out of your home.

"*Azure, I'm leaving.*"

He freezes, carefully placing his tablet back onto the desk, and looking Ocher in the eye. "*What do you mean?*"

"*I can't live here anymore.*"

"*Yes, you can.*"

"*No,*" *Ocher shakes his head.* "*I don't learn anything here.*"

Azure stands and comes around the desk to face him. "*Learn? What do you need to learn? I'll teach you.*"

"*That's what I mean! You already take care of everything. I want to find out who I am...without you.*"

He stares into determined gray eyes, the same eyes that used to always follow him around and question him. What is happening? Has he not spent an entire year ensuring that Ocher only thinks of him? That he wants for nothing and has no problems? Now, he's saying he wants independence? *Unacceptable.*

"*Are you coming back?*"

"*I don't know.*"

"*You don't know? Let me answer that for you then, don't bother.*" *Ocher knows better than to think he can just wander in and out his life as freely as he wants.*

"*Azure, don't say that.*"

"*Why shouldn't I? Your word clearly means nothing. It's worthless just like you.*"

Ocher takes a breath, "*I know you're just mad at me right now.*"

"*You're not worth being mad over.*"

"*Azure.*"

"Leave then. Go get the independence you want so much and don't show your face here again."

"It's not that I want to leave you," Ocher protests.

"Except that's exactly what it is."

"You just don't give me choices. You only want me to care about you, there's no room for anything else."

"So? That's nothing new. You knew that when you agreed. If you didn't think you could do it, then you shouldn't have agreed! You're a liar."

"You're more of a liar than I could ever be!"

"Good thing you're leaving."

"Azure, I-"

"No!" Azure grabs him by the arm and drags him towards the door. "You're a liar and you've made your choice. I don't want or need someone like you around. Go out there and die for all I care, which you probably will. At least it'll be your *mistake." He shoves him across the threshold, "Get out. Don't come back. We're through."*

He hadn't taken their separation well. The minute he realized Ocher was leaving him, he'd checked out to avoid the hurt. It's why he never lets anyone get that close and the one person he did, still left.

It's no wonder Ocher never tried to come back, he'd made it very clear back then that he was unwelcome if he left. Maybe his expectations were unreasonable, but Ocher never should have told him yes if he wasn't sure.

Who knows what was going through his mind that entire year they were together? Was he just biding his time until he decided to leave? Did he even care? He hadn't asked those questions then and he doesn't want to know the answer now either. That kind of uncertainty is why he doesn't do relationships, but stupidly he'd let the stray soldier he picked up become part of him.

Now look where that's gotten them.

He throws the last of their supplies into the back of the vehicle and turns to find Ocher regarding him warily. Gray eyes are latched onto him and when they meet, Ocher shifts back, posture becoming closed off and guarded. What's he nervous about now? *Now,* he doesn't want to be alone together?

Ocher's gaze flickers away and he hates the feeling that arises within him, possessiveness, a need to bully him until he opens up again. The need to coddle him afterwards. The affection he feels when Ocher looks at him that way, uncertain and questioning with just a hint of longing, is far too familiar. Azure has always disliked how expressive his eyes are.

And suddenly, he can't stand it anymore.

He corners Ocher, forcing him backwards until he's pinned against the truck, and watching him blink in surprise. There won't be any interruptions this time, Basel is occupying the freeloaders. "So, did you find that independence you so desperately wanted?"

Ocher pushes at his arm and it's futile, he won't be able to move him, even though he knows Ocher thinks it's unfair when he uses his extra strength. "Maybe I did."

"There's no maybe. Did you or not?"

"Fine, yes! I survived on my own for a year even when you didn't think I could!"

"I never said I didn't think you could," Azure corrects. "I said we'd be better off together and that you were making a mistake."

"Except clearly I didn't."

"And are you happy? Which one of them are you going to pick?"

"Who says I'm going to pick either one? I don't have to."

"You're just going to lead them on? Yeah, you are pretty good at that," Azure mocks. "Dragging people along with false promises."

"Move out of the way, Azure. We have nothing to do with them. *You're* the one who told me not to ever come back."

"I just wanted you to have all the freedom you could stand."

"And I did," Ocher replies, crossing his arms. "So what are you mad about? I did what you wanted."

"Are you *happy?*" He presses again.

"What do you want me to say? Yes, I'm happy. I have a home. Yes, it's a home!" He repeats at Azure's scoff. "I have friends, a job, a whole life and you're not a part of it! Yes, I'm happy!"

Azure kisses him, surging forward to seal their lips together and silence him. He doesn't want to hear those words whether Ocher means them or not. Ocher kisses him back and Azure knows that he'll eventually force the truth out of him.

He pulls back, "Okay. You can have all the independence you want. It's yours for the taking, we're just five people traveling together." Azure walks around to the passenger side at Basel's arrival and tosses him the keys. "You drive now."

Basel takes the keys with a shake of his head, "You two always bring out the worst in each other."

CHAPTER 4: OCHER

"Azure, pull over here. I'm hungry." Basel tells him, and Ocher's grateful for another break when Azure listens.

It's been a long drive, squeezed between Eren and Erina and listening to Azure and Basel banter back and forth for hours. Oddly enough, the relationship between him and Azure never reached that level. Maybe it's because they were never friends. They skipped that stage entirely.

He does his best not to show how much the ease of Basel and Azure's relationship bothers him, aware of how the twins are always watching and trying to read his reactions. Basel and Azure were close before he ever entered the picture and he knows that he should respect that, but he doesn't like when he's second, which he can easily become when Basel is around.

Sometimes he's just as bad as Azure.

"Did you go through the supply of food you bought already?"

"Nope," Basel answers, pushing open his door. "But a guy I met a few weeks ago said this country has good food and when am I going to come this way again?"

"On the way back," Azure replies.

Basel makes a face, "Then we can eat here twice. Come on before they close!"

The four of them trail after Basel and with only a brief hesitation, Ocher grabs Azure's wrist and pulls him back. "Can I talk to you?" He's already mentally prepared for Azure to be a jerk about it, but he can't go the entire trip being ignored. If he does, then coming along was pointless. There's no future for them. Just because Azure kissed him doesn't mean there was any affection behind it or that he would take him back.

Azure stops, "Do you want to talk or do you want to lie to me some more?"

"I didn't lie."

"Then you're happy and there's nothing you need to talk to me about."

Ocher's hand tightens on his wrist, pulling him back before he can turn away. "I can be happy and still want more."

"That sounds greedy of you."

"You've always been greedy with me."

"Have I? From what I remember, I didn't want anything to do with you and you forced yourself into my life."

"After that."

"After that, you said you wanted to leave and I didn't stop you. That's the opposite of greedy.

Ocher makes a sound of frustration, "You know exactly what I'm talking about! You demanded everything of me, I'm allowed to want things too."

"Yes, you are. Want as much as you like, but I don't have to agree with it."

"If you're not going to forgive me, then you never should have come to find me. I was fine where I was."

"Do you want me to forgive you?"

"I don't think I deserve your anger. I didn't do anything wrong, but if you're mad, then yes, I want to be forgiven."

Azure rolls his eyes and pulls his wrist free. "That was the worst apology I've ever heard from you. You used to be better at them. Do whatever you want Ocher. I can't control you."

"Why am I here if you don't want me back?" He shouts.

"I don't know," Azure shrugs. "Why *are* you here? When you figure it out, let me know."

Azure walks away to join the others inside who are all unsubtly watching them from the window and Ocher goes the other way, back inside their truck. He stretches out across the backseat and stares up at the grey fabric of the ceiling.

If Azure cared enough to seek him out after an entire year, there must still be something there. The problem is that Azure is stubborn and holds a grudge. Azure *does* want something from him, it just takes so much effort to placate him. The only way to break through that is to make Azure want him, it's the only time he's even somewhat open to compromise.

He wants to go home and he's not sure which of the two he means.

"Ocher?" Erina peers in at him. "Do you want us to bring you something?"

"No, I'm not hungry."

"Are you sure? That other guy says we're not stopping again."

"I'll survive."

She frowns, "If you don't want to go anymore. I'm sure the three of us can find a way back. We don't have to go with them."

Maybe they don't, but he does. If he picked the two of them over Azure, he would never be allowed back in Haithen ever again. Azure would have both the power and the anger to ban him if he did something like that. They don't understand, Azure isn't someone you want to piss off. He doesn't have to be in a bad mood to do terrible things.

Ocher pulls himself up and forces a smile, "It's fine. I'm just tired.

Once we sleep, I'll feel better."

"If you say so." She slides in beside him as the others return. Azure doesn't even spare him a glance before he starts driving again. It hurts.

Maybe he should have given in the moment Azure showed up.

◆ ◆ ◆

A few hours after sunset, they reach the base of the mountains bordering Vita. In front of them is the shadowed craggy outline of the mountains and in the dark, it's impossible to see the way forward.

"Should we stop here for the night and start up tomorrow?" Basel asks.

"That works. I'd rather attempt the mountains in the daytime anyway," Azure answers.

They all climb out of the vehicle and immediately he's shivering from the temperature change. The twins press in next to him, none of them realized how low the temperature had dropped while they were inside.

Azure drops a tent at their feet and begins setting up his own, heedless of their discomfort.

"We're just going to sleep here, *outside?*"

Azure spares Erina a fleeting glance, "What did you think I bought tents for?"

"Not to sleep on a mountain!"

"Technically, we haven't gone up the mountain. Basel, I'm not setting up your tent, so don't wait for it." Azure looks at them, "Yours either."

Wait a minute. He had assumed Basel would be in his own, the twins in another, and him with Azure, but maybe not. As if sensing his thoughts, Azure looks back at him, "You're not sleeping in my tent, Ocher."

"Why not?"

Azure shrugs, "Exert that independence. You're with them."

"But they already have two people in theirs."

"So? You're all friends, squeeze in tight. I like to sleep *independently.*"

His jaw tightens. Why did he even expect otherwise? "Fine." He grabs the tent and moves away to set it up, he won't give Azure the satisfaction of protesting.

They can't leave any type of fire burning out here while they sleep, so once they all head inside their respective tents he's incredibly grateful that Azure cared enough to give them several thick blankets. Otherwise they really might have had to squeeze together for warmth, not that it would have been hard in their small tent.

By the time they've settled in for the night, there's only a few inches separating them, but it's warm enough to sleep. He falls asleep easily, ready for morning to come.

The next morning, he's the first one awake and wiggling his way out of the tent just in time to see Basel leaving Azure's tent. He freezes. They can't be. Unless they got together in the year he was gone? Azure had kissed him though, *twice.* Maybe Basel doesn't care? He wouldn't be surprised. Basel has always taken most things in stride.

Ocher sucks in a sharp breath of the cold, morning air, letting it settle heavily in his lungs. He's not going to let this upset him, there's no way to know for sure if that's why Basel was there, and if it was, no one would care how he felt about it.

He never asked Azure if he and Basel were together before. If they were, falling back into a casual routine would be a simple thing for them. What he hopes is that they were just cold. Previously that would have been him, he thinks bitterly. Instead, Azure has made it clear that Ocher's place is no longer by his side.

They pack up and leave after a dry breakfast, loading into the truck and powering up the mountain. There's not much of a road anymore once they get higher up. They're jostled over the mounds of snow and hidden branches in their path crunch under the wheels.

It's slow going with no direction except up and Ocher thinks maybe they should have planned this better, asked how people traversed the mountain instead of assuming a giant truck would be enough. Silence falls between them as snow flurries gently drift by outside the windows. There's nothing much to say after being stuck together and watching the same view for hours.

Near dusk, they take a break to decide whether to make camp or keep going. The first thing he realizes when his foot sinks into the ground is that he's woefully unprepared for this. The snow is beautiful and more than he's ever seen before, but it's also freezing and soaking into his pants and shoes.

He's not enjoying it.

The twins like it though. They throw snowballs at each other and laugh. Ocher shoves his hands into his pockets and stomps back through the snow to the vehicle before they can involve him. He's almost there when he's hit with coldness on the back of his head that immediately melts into water dripping down his back.

Ocher turns and finds Azure smirking at him, holding another snowball. So, it's going to be one of those times. He reaches for the door handle and of course, it's locked. Another snowball hits him in the back, and then they come one after the other until he's soaked through.

"Azure!"

"What?" He says innocently. "I thought you wanted to have a snowball fight."

He sneezes. "I'm soaked!"

"Yeah," he agrees. "They all melted pretty fast. Who knew that would happen?"

They both know the answer to that. Azure probably *only* threw them because he could melt them right away. Far sneakier than openly pouring water on him to show his annoyance with him right now.

"You're such a jerk," he shivers.

"At least my mouth isn't turning blue," Azure retorts, walking away. "Ask Eren to warm you up, I'm sure he'd love that."

Ignoring his own rapidly stiffening limbs, Ocher scoops up his own snowball and throws it at Azure's back. He's not the least bit surprised when it slows midway and reverses, smashing him in the face to the sound of Azure's laughter.

For a second he forgot that he *never* wins against Azure.

Azure is on him in a second, pinning him into the snow and rubbing another cold snowball into his face. "Azure, stop!" He gasps out past the snow melting into his mouth.

"Sorry, what's that? I can't hear you."

"You can!" Ocher shoves helplessly at him. His face is freezing, his hands are starting to ache, and he's choking on snow. "Stop!" He knees Azure in the stomach, but rather than pull back, Azure collapses on him with a grunt, forcing him deeper into the snow. He can't feel anything below his ankles anymore. "Get off me."

"I think you really hurt me. I'm not sure I can move."

"It takes more than that to hurt you, *move.*"

Azure makes a pathetic, and he knows completely fake, sound of pain, "Kiss it better?"

"*No.* I can't even feel my face, thanks to you."

"Hm," Azure props himself up on one arm and presses the slightest kiss against the corner of his mouth, sending a burst of heat through him to chase away the worst of the cold.

He blinks up at Azure without making any movement to go further, and Azure stares back wordlessly. Ocher sighs and looks away, Azure is going to be the one to determine their boundaries, as always. For a while, he could cross them without a care. He's lost that privilege.

"Azure, come on!" Basel shouts at them. "Leave him alone and help us see if there's shelter around here where we can stay the night!"

Azure pushes himself back to his feet, perfectly fine as he'd assumed, and he immediately misses his closeness. The twins stare at him from their spot huddled together near the truck, the cold has gotten to them now too.

He's squeezing his clothes out in the dying light of the evening sun and watching Azure scout the area when he sees Azure freeze, then start heading back to the truck. He opens his mouth to question what's wrong, but the sounds reach him first. Deep growls of a wild animal and the crunch of something heavy on snow.

The first creature steps out from the trees and Basel fires at it without hesitating. The shot goes over the creature's head and does nothing except cause three more to appear.

Then Azure is running back towards them, grabbing his arm in one hand and Basel's in the other, and hauling them towards the truck. He practically throws the two of them inside and climbs in after them.

The three of them are tangled across the front seats as the first impact shakes the vehicle. The creatures snarl as they prowl around the truck, seeing prey, but unable to reach them.

Azure is pressed against him, watching through the window as the creatures charge the truck at different points to check for weaknesses and Ocher can't help turning his head, pressing his mouth to the softness of Azure's hair.

Azure shoves him into Basel without a backwards glance. "Thankfully, this thing is reinforced. Why do you have a gun, Basel?"

"There's no way I'm going somewhere unfamiliar without protection. Especially not a place that so many people ran from," Basel answers, shoving him off as well. They rearrange themselves and somehow he still ends up straddling Azure's lap.

"I vote for turning back," Basel says.

Azure shakes his head, "We already came this far, there's no way we're turning back."

"Are you seeing this? Who knows what else could be out there!"

Ocher peers out the window. The creatures are larger than wolves with long canines extending from their mouths into sharp points. Their fur is thick and white to help them blend in with their surroundings, but their dark eyes gleam with intelligence. These creatures understand the long game and when they win, there's no mercy for their prey.

One lets out a low growl when it sees Ocher's eyes on it and he shifts away from the window, letting Azure steady him with a hand on his waist.

"Maybe they're only this feral because no one else comes through here and they're not used to humans," Azure guesses. "That doesn't mean it's any more dangerous than mountains back in Haithen."

"They're also huge," Basel adds plainly.

"Evolution."

"I'm not getting out of the truck again." Ocher silently agrees with Basel's complaint. He doesn't want to be caught off guard and ripped apart either. Returning to Haithen sounds like the better plan to him.

Eventually, when they can't find any weakness in the truck's armor, the creatures give up and slink away. It's only then that he realizes he's still soaked as he shivers in Azure's lap.

"You're going to get sick."

Ocher glares down at Azure, "And whose fault is that?"

Azure peels his soaked jacket off and Ocher lifts his arms to help him get the shirt over his head. With those two layers gone, he feels warmer already. Gentle fingers run along his stomach, tracing along the muscles there and when Azure looks up, their gazes lock and stay locked as Azure's hand moves to explore up his chest.

There's heat in the way Azure's darkened eyes stare into his own and he shudders involuntarily under the press of warm fingers against his cold skin. The look in Azure's eyes says *mine* and at that moment, Ocher can't remember why he ever thought life would be better apart.

"If you two get any grosser, I'll throw you out of here myself."

Azure looks away from him and he's disappointed. That could have been a chance to make Azure really want him again.

"He's cold, Basel."

"I think we can *all* tell that."

Azure shrugs and pulls Ocher into the circle of his arms, pressing them together, so he can feel the blazing heat of him against his bare skin, chasing away the chill.

An uncomfortable cough drags his attention to the backseat and he looks over Azure's shoulder to see the twin's shaken expressions.

"Are you two okay?"

"Yeah, we're fine," Erina answers for them. They're lucky they reacted in time or they would have been goners. Azure wouldn't have spared a thought to save them.

"Are you regretting coming?"

"A little."

"No choice now," Azure interrupts and pushes Ocher away to lift towards the back seat, so he can retake his spot between two of them. "Unless you want to wait for them to come back, guess we're driving overnight."

"Guess so," Basel agrees, sending him a dirty look. "And I assume we're going forwards and not backwards?"

"You would be correct."

"Killed by wild animals," he mutters.

"Miss your tower, huh?"

"Just drive, Azure."

They start moving again with the front lights on full brightness as they creep slowly through the mountain on the lookout for anything that might damage the truck if run over. No one wants to get stranded out here. There's no rescue.

Sometime around midnight, he dozes off and wakes to full sunlight with a head on each of his shoulders. Azure is asleep now and Basel is driving, so they must have kept driving all night.

Morning is the best time of day to observe Azure, not to speak to him because he's definitely not a morning person, but it's perfect for catching him exposed, when his posture is less guarded and all the tense lines of his face are smoothed out.

He reaches out a tentative hand to touch him and Basel's voice cuts him off, "Hands to yourself, runaway."

"What? I didn't run away, I was kicked out."

"Same difference," Basel waves his argument away. "People who disappear for a year don't get to do whatever they want when they come back."

"What does it matter to you?"

"Whether you're around or not, he's still my friend. That doesn't change no matter how much *your* feelings do. Keep your hands to yourself, if you want to touch, wait until he's awake and can say yes."

Ocher sits back, Azure's not going to agree once he's awake.

By the time they descend to the base of the mountains, everyone else is awake too, and they stop for a short break before continuing on. Near late morning, they reach the first town in Vita. It's small and slightly shabby, but everyone jumps out, eager to stretch after hours trapped inside.

"There's no internet here," Azure states, checking his tablet. "Isn't this the perfect set up? A mountain full of feral animals to cross and no internet to call for help once you get here."

Basel glowers, "We should have turned back when we had the chance."

"Hopefully we won't need to be here long. Let's find out where we are."

Eren runs off ahead, unaware of how dangerous that could be in an unfamiliar place, and the rest of them follow at a slower pace.

They don't get past more than a few houses before a boy approaches them hesitantly. "How did you get here? You came from the mountain and no one was eaten?"

Basel shoves to the front of their group. "People *know* about those animals? Do something about them!" He demands.

The boy shakes his head, "They're to keep people from crossing the mountains, they're not going anywhere."

"I can already see why people left. Who are you anyway?"

"I'm Ciaran," the boy introduces himself and Ocher looks him over. He's pale and slight with curious dark brown eyes and short black hair. Maybe a year or two younger than him.

"Basel. We're from Haithen and here to speak with whoever's in charge of this country."

Ciaran takes the sight of them in with no small amount of surprise, "You want to meet our leaders? I don't...think they meet just anyone. They don't like outsiders here. Maybe you should go back."

"Not on your life. We came too far. Besides, we're not just anyone. We're representatives of Haithen's leadership," Basel replies, gesturing between himself and Azure. "We need to at least speak with someone before we head home."

"I can show you the way," Ciaran begins unsurely. "But, I can't guarantee they'll see you."

"Fine, we'll do the rest."

It's then that Ocher notices that Azure hasn't spoken, leaving Basel to explain everything in his stead. In fact, he hasn't taken his eyes off Ciaran, his gaze is strangely intense on him and Ocher feels that ugly curl of jealousy building up in his stomach again.

Ciaran looks to Azure and he flushes when their eyes meet, red rising in his cheeks under the attention. Ocher doesn't like that, at all.

"It's a little far to the capital and you all look like you need a rest. We don't have a hotel, but there's somewhere you can stay."

"Okay."

Ciaran guides them to a house larger than the rest and the entire time he can see Azure's eyes boring into his back. Ocher studies the other boy. He can't see the appeal of Ciaran, definitely not for that type of attention, but he also has to admit that he doesn't know exactly what Azure's type is.

He should ask Sera the next time they see each other.

Ciaran knocks on the worn brown door and an old lady answers, looking more wary than welcoming to see them.

"We don't get many visitors," Ciaran explains and introduces the woman as Myrta, the de facto leader of their small town. Her home doubles as the town's meeting space and guest rooms for anyone who may come through.

She seats them around a long communal table and begins preparing a meal while simultaneously ignoring any of their questions, leaving them to Ciaran.

"Is every town like this?" Basel asks.

Ciaran turns to him, "Like what?"

"Small and shabby with no people."

"We have people. They just keep to themselves. And no, the other towns aren't all like ours, we're just near the outskirts."

"So the rest are fine?"

Ciaran hesitates. "Yes."

"Then why do people leave and never want to come back here?"

Myrta slams a bowl down on the table, cutting off whatever Ciaran was going to say. "Enough questions! Don't come here questioning our country. If I remember correctly, your country was ruled by fear and the military until recently. I'm sure your citizens wanted out as well!"

"She's not wrong," Erina murmurs.

Ciaran shrugs apologetically, "It's best not to ask too many questions, leads to trouble. The only place you might get answers is the capital."

Basel huffs and turns to the bowl being shoved in front of him. Ocher looks into his own bowl. It's red and full of vegetables, no meat at all. He takes a bite and grimaces. It's both sweet and hot at the same time, and very very thick.

He pushes the bowl away and that's a testament to how spoiled he's gotten because before he would have eaten whatever was put in front of him with no preference.

His gaze turns back to Ciaran and his annoyance grows at how the entire time they eat, Ciaran and Azure's eyes flick towards each other. Even Basel raises an eyebrow at how obvious they are.

He's jealous. Azure never responded to him that way when they first met.

Ciaran clears his throat, "After you rest, if you want...I can lead you to the capital." He says it to all of them, but he's looking at Azure.

"Yes," Azure answers quickly.

"I think we can find it ourselves," Ocher disagrees. He doesn't want Ciaran around any longer than he needs to be.

Basel laughs, "We're in an unfamiliar place with no map. We're definitely taking his offer."

"There's no room," Ocher insists.

"You'll just have to squeeze together."

"That doesn't make sense, we don't - "

"He's coming," Azure cuts him off firmly.

Myrta looks between them and decides not to ask. She stands, "I have two rooms you can rest in. You can figure out the arrangements yourselves."

Ocher moves to claim Azure first, but Basel is there blocking him. "No, I'm sleeping with Azure."

"Don't touch me," Ocher snaps, shaking his arm off.

Basel shrugs and points at the other room before grabbing Azure by the arm, startling him out of his staring, and hauling him into the first room. The door shuts behind them with a decisive click.

Ocher seethes, he hates Basel more every time he sees him and who's this new boy? He turns on him and Ciaran flinches back at the vehemence of his gaze.

Part of him wishes he had never come while another part whispers that then he wouldn't be here to keep them apart. He hates the thought, yet he still has to wonder how many people there have been since he's been gone.

He joins Eren and Erina in the second room. It holds a decent sized bed, but with the three of them, it's still going to be a tight fit and he refuses to sleep in the middle again. Azure wouldn't care if he had to sleep close to Basel and the certainty of that knowledge annoys him more.

The twins talk about everything that's happened so far, nothing he cares to discuss. At one point, they even mention Azure's interest in Ciaran and Ocher forces himself not to react. He has a mask to keep in place, no matter how quickly it's beginning to fall apart.

"I'm tired," is the excuse he gives when he curls up on the edge of the bed. Their voices lower to a whisper behind him and Ocher tries his hardest to shut them out.

CHAPTER 5: AZURE

"Okay, what's the crazy fascination with the boy?" Basel demands to know as soon as the door shuts behind them.

"What do you mean?"

"Don't play dumb. You've barely taken your eyes off him since we saw him."

"I think he has abilities."

"What?"

"I don't know," Azure shrugs. "But I can feel something from him."

Basel raises a skeptical eyebrow, "Abilities like yours?"

"Yes."

"And, what, you're happy you met someone else like you?"

He shakes his head, "Not exactly. More like...you know how I said I was draining fast?"

"Yeah..." Basel answers, expression growing wary.

"I think it can be replenished. A lot of me is drawn to his energy. I think my body wants to drain him, badly."

"Just to be clear, we're still talking about his energy, right?"

Azure rolls his eyes. "Yes. I'm not positive, but I think it would help me heal or it feels like it anyway. It's like a charged hum, sort of an attraction, but not physically. My energy pulls towards his in hunger."

"So, what will you do?"

"Nothing for now. I can't just jump on him."

"True." Basel smirks, "Not to mention, I'm sure your brat would have a problem with that."

Azure waves his words away. "Ocher is occupied with those twins, too busy trying to make sure his facade doesn't fall apart. He's not worried about me."

Basel gives him a blank stare and shakes his head, sighing loudly. "I know you don't believe that or he wouldn't be here."

"He has his moments, but he wants his independence. He should be happy that I'm letting him have it."

"Moments? Azure, please. You've spoiled him so rotten that he can't take not being the center of your attention."

"He can be a brat sometimes," Azure admits. "But he's no worse than me."

"Uh huh."

"He's always felt threatened by you and doesn't like you near me."

"Then how's he going to react to you all over Ciaran?"

"First, I'm not going to be all over Ciaran. I said it's not physical. Also, he's grown past that."

"You're such a liar. Earlier he looked like he wanted to rip Ciaran's head off. You would know if you could look away from him for a single second."

Azure laughs dismissively. "He looks at you the same way, but he never does."

"Still, do something about it! Your usual coddling or whatever, this is going to be an even longer trip if he's like that the whole time."

He shakes his head in refusal, "He'll just have to be upset, I can't be soft with him anymore."

"And why not?" Basel demands. "You've never had a problem with it before."

"He takes advantage if I'm soft with him."

Basel regards him skeptically, "What? How is that?"

"He's shady. You don't get it. If I give even an inch, he'll pry his way back in. He would definitely run me over."

"So, he's like you?"

"No," Azure glares. "I'm up front about it."

Basel rolls his eyes, "How could he *possibly* take advantage of you when you already give him anything and everything he wants?"

"I don't anymore."

Basel sighs, "Whatever happened with you two that entire year? It's clear he doesn't hate you."

"What happened...nothing much."

"Was it that bad?"

"No, it was pretty good. You should ask him about it sometime."

Basel shoots him another skeptical look and shoves him aside. "I already know better than to believe anything that comes out of your mouth regarding him." He stretches out across the bed, leaving only a sliver of space. "Stop talking. I don't want to hear any more of your lies."

Azure sits on the edge of the bed, debating. He knows he should try to get some rest too, but he's wired. He can feel the thrum of Ciaran's energy under his skin and he knows exactly which direction he's in. The constant awareness agitates him.

It's different from Ocher. Ocher's presence is like a gentle pull on his heart, a part of him that he can always find his way back to and when he does, coming together is always seamless.

The new pull is insistent and can't be ignored, probably his body's inherent want to survive.

If he's being honest, he's not sure he can resist Ciaran and deal with Ocher's emotions at the same time. It's taking all his will to keep from draining Ciaran dry and he's well aware that the longer all of them are together, the worse Ocher will get.

People are exhausting.

◆ ◆ ◆

By early evening, they're prepared to leave. If Ciaran's correct, they should make it to the capital shortly after dawn provided nothing goes wrong.

Basel grabs the keys from him, "I'll take the first shift."

"You drove last."

He looks at the five of them, "I can already see where this is going and I'll drive."

"He's got a point," Eren agrees. "How will we all fit?"

Easy. "Ciaran can sit up here with me," Azure answers.

"No!"

He sighs, ignoring Basel's low laughter. That would be Ocher, disagreeable as he always seems to be now. "Yes. Unless the four of you want to be smashed together back there the whole trip, this is better." And maybe he can drain a little energy through their close proximity.

"No! That's too long. I don't want him to sit up there!"

It would help Ocher so much if he knew how to come up with some type of reasoning on why it's a bad idea. Instead, how he feels is what he chooses to lean on. Lying will never be his strong suit.

"I'm not going to stand here and argue with you," Azure says.

"Okay." He folds his arms and stares back. "Leave then. I'm not going."

"So what, you're just going to stay here all alone?"

He shrugs, "Yeah."

Azure turns away, "Looks like a seat just opened up. Everybody in, let's go."

"You're seriously going to leave him here?" Basel looks between the two of them. "Is that a good idea?"

"Ocher can handle himself." He's yanking open the passenger door when he's suddenly assaulted by a barrage of emotions, anger, sadness, jealousy, loneliness, hostility. It's enough to send his head spinning.

His eyes move directly to Ocher who's glaring back at him with just a hint of smugness in his expression. Did he just…? He really just used their connection against him. When did he learn to do that? Ocher shouldn't be able to, unless he's weakened even more and the subconscious protection to keep Ocher out of his head and their emotions separate is fading.

He needs those few moments alone with Ciaran even more. This type of vulnerability is too much for him to deal with right now.

Another barrage of emotions hits him, this time harder, heavier, and sustained. Now he *knows* it's on purpose and he can tell that Ocher is going to fight until he gets what he wants.

Apparently he's not deciding fast enough because a third attack comes more aggressive than the second and this time his vision darkens.

"Ocher!" Azure reaches out and grabs him, just to get him to stop the assault. Once his fingers wrap around Ocher's wrist, it's a simple thing to force the connection closed, however temporary it might be. And then there's peace inside his own head again.

Azure shoves him into the passenger seat and climbs in after him. Part of him still can't believe he lost. That never happens. He looks down to where Ocher is pressed against him and finds him already looking back with self-satisfied eyes. "You're annoying."

"Don't care." Ocher replies, pressing closer to him in the small space.

"For someone so averse to sex, you have no problem climbing all over me."

"Different things," he says and slips his fingers under Azure's shirt.

Azure grabs his wrist and pushes his hand away. "Don't."

"*Why?* You always did!"

He looks away. Big gray eyes and a pout, together they're two of his greatest weaknesses. "I always took more liberties than you did. Besides, it's not like we're dating, or ever were. Keep your hands to yourself." He ignores Ocher's glare. "Your words, not mine."

Basel hops into the driver's seat and shoots him a knowing look. "I told you so."

"You're annoying too." And even if Basel's right, it's not all Ocher's fault. He gave his attention freely in the past, so why shouldn't Ocher be used to it and want it back on him? That was the whole point of devoting so much time to Ocher, to keep him near.

Then he left anyway.

He exhales in frustration, ignoring the curious look Ocher gives him. He's tired and dealing with Ocher is draining in a way he doesn't remember it being previously.

Perhaps it's because of Ciaran's presence or maybe because he wants Ocher back the way they were before, when things were easy and there weren't so many different factors. Or maybe he's dying and *everything* seems like a struggle now.

It's not really fair of him to pull Ocher back to him when he knows he doesn't have much time left, but he's never claimed to be unselfish. Even though at times, Ocher feels like a stranger, he still wants him near in his last days.

His only regret would've been dying without putting things to rest between them. Azure isn't sure there's a future for them anymore. Ocher may want his attention, but it seems like that's only because he's around. Once they've gone their separate ways, Ocher won't care anymore and even if he wasn't dying, that's too much.

Half-hearted caring is something he will never accept and Ocher should know that.

But no matter what happens, he's started this. So now he'll see it through to the end.

They're crossing into the capital boundary when Ciaran leans forward and points out a light in the distance down the single lane road. "That's a checkpoint. No one gets any closer to the capital without stopping there."

"And what happens there?" Basel asks, easing off the gas.

"They ask a few questions and check the vehicle."

"So, what are we supposed to say?"

"What do you mean?"

"Isn't there some lie or story to help us get through?"

"Tell the truth?" Ciaran suggests. "I don't come to the capital that often, but they don't hate visitors. Some people never leave. It's safe there."

"Sure it is," Basel mutters. "So safe that you choose to live near a mountain with feral animals."

Ciaran sighs. "I'm used to it, it's my home. Besides I wouldn't have gotten to meet you all from Haithen if I lived in the capital. And you wouldn't have met me!"

"Well, aren't we just the luckiest."

"Basel, be nice." Azure interrupts and immediately feels the annoyance rolling off Ocher. "To both of them," he corrects.

Basel smirks as the truck rolls to a stop. He lets down the window and at least four guys surround them, makes sense when they're in such a large, army vehicle.

They're ordered out for their vehicle to be searched and Azure leaves the answering of questions to Basel. He's better with words anyway. He wanders over to the only building open at this time of night. It's a small understocked store carrying only a few necessities with an overabundance of hot, finger food.

This is probably the only store for miles and all their money likely comes from travelers and feeding the guards. He wouldn't eat any of this, though someone else would.

Azure selects a single seasoned kebab, still steaming from the grill and shiny with oil. The one lady manning the counter glares suspiciously at his money, but relents and waves him away without accepting it.

He nods his thanks, stepping back outside to rejoin the group and of course, Ocher who moves in close as soon as he comes back. "Open."

Ocher wrinkles his nose, "I don't like when you tell me that."

"So? Do it anyway."

"I don't - "

Azure pushes the food into his open mouth, "You talk too much now."

He pulls the kebab free, "What is this?"

"Something you'll actually eat." Despite what they think, he can pay attention to more than one thing at a time and he's aware Ocher didn't eat. He's particular and the food was too different for him. "Don't start."

Ocher is staring back at him with surprised eyes, like he's about to get emotional and Azure walks away before it can get to that point. Paying attention to him isn't a new thing and Ocher should be used to it, but he supposes a year made him forget that too.

They've passed the inspection when he reaches Basel and he offers to drive the rest of the way. Basel's onboard until he glances back and catches sight of Ocher, then he retracts his agreement, unwilling to argue about seating arrangements.

Azure laughs, "You don't want to sit with him?"

"Not a chance in hell. One of us wouldn't make it."

They drive throughout the rest of the night. For the most part, it's a dark, silent trip with no cars out and deserted streets when they pass through a city. Ciaran mentions something about a curfew with strict consequences for breaking it and that makes sense.

Hours later, the second barricade stops them. No vehicles are allowed past that point and they must continue on foot. Basel parks where they're directed and they grab their bags to head down the dirt path towards the capital.

Morning is quiet and cool with just the smallest hint of moisture in the air. He's rarely up early enough to experience the peace of an early morning.

The siblings join Ocher on either side and Azure brightens, using Ocher's temporary distraction as an opportunity to fall into step with Ciaran and maybe get some answers.

"Was that woman from before your grandmother?"

"No," Ciaran answers. "She was just in charge of the area. It's only a small town. The first place when you arrive and the last place before the mountains. We don't get many visitors and since she's in charge, she has the biggest house. If visitors need somewhere to stay, she's the best option."

"Then, didn't you need to ask your family if you could come with us?"

"I don't have family there."

"You're an orphan?"

"Not...necessarily. I have family, just not there."

Azure raises an eyebrow. "Do you hate your family?" He asks bluntly.

"No!"

"It's fine if you do. Ocher doesn't like his either."

"It's not that I don't like them, I don't really know them." He leans in and drops his voice, "I'm actually illegitimate from the royal family. They sent me to that little town when I was a child. Probably to keep me out of sight."

Royalty? Is that what they're dealing with here? There was nothing about royalty in the brief research he did. Then again, that information was decades old.

If Ciaran's illegitimate that means that someone at the capital is an enchanter and it'll be interesting to find out how they got from Ustrina to here. He's sure he'll be able to sense who. Even with his weakness, the pull of an enchanter's energy is always noticeable, just like with Ciaran.

"And you've never wanted to come back here and find out who your parents are?"

"I was curious, yeah, but they sent me away for a reason. I don't think they'd welcome me back with open arms. Besides, it's hard to get from my small town to the capital. People aren't making that trip everyday."

"I guess it's good that we came along then."

Ciaran flashes him a smile. "I'm appreciative at least."

"Incoming," Basel mutters from behind them.

Azure looks up to see Ocher glaring daggers at the two of them. If looks could kill, Ciaran would be dead twice over. Still, it's Ocher's own fault and he'll have to learn to deal with that. When he knows what he wants, he knows what he has to do.

"Is there a problem?" Azure calls out. "Perhaps something you want to say to me," he goads when the other boy turns back around. "Eren, Erina, I don't think you're keeping him interested. Maybe try a hug, it looks like he needs one."

"Azure!"

"What? It was only a suggestion, Ocher. You look a little tense. If you don't want one from them, you can come back here. I'm open."

His eyes flick to Ciaran and back to him before he speeds up. Azure laughs quietly. Ocher's such a brat.

Soon enough they reach the city limits and it's a lot cheerier than he expected for the amount of armed guards protecting the place. Even more unexpected is that no one seems ill or hurt. Everyone looks healthy.

They walk through the streets and interestingly enough, he can see faint traces of Ustrina's architecture in the buildings which confirms that some of his people made it here. The city streets are wide, full of people moving by.

There are no street stalls or people mingling outside. The city is pristine and every street is lined with buildings in the same color and shape. Not much diversity, but the city seems to be run like a well oiled machine.

He could see how the structure might chafe a bit after a while, not enough for him to live in a caravan though. Organization over roughing it anyday.

Most people don't pay them any mind, so the few that stare at them as they walk by are especially noticeable. He's not sure exactly what it is, but something marks them as outsiders.

The capitol building is easy to see, looming against the skyline on the opposite side of the city.

Next to him, Ciaran looks excited, absorbing every part of their surroundings and Azure has to wonder if he ever left his tiny town near the mountains. This could be the farthest he's ever been from home.

The building is a welcome sight, he's tired of traveling and ready to settle down for a while. He grabs Ciaran's wrist and shoves past the rest of their group to pick up the pace. They can introduce themselves, find somewhere to stay, and he can sleep for the next twelve hours in a bed.

He sets a fast pace through the street and people go out of their way to avoid them. As they get closer to the capitol, the stares increase and it's starting to get annoying. Have these people really never had visitors? He wouldn't be surprised considering they don't even speak or seem all that welcoming.

The capitol is a bronze tower, reaching fifteen stories into the air and eclipsing every other building in the vicinity. There's no gate surrounding it and only two guards at the entrance.

Azure marches up to them with Ciaran in tow and announces himself. "I'm a representative from Haithen here to discuss relations between our two countries and the amount of immigrants coming our way. This is the rest of my delegation," he gestures behind him vaguely. "Who do we need to speak to?"

The first man blinks in surprise and the two guards share a look. "You crossed the mountains to get here?"

"Yes, it wasn't that difficult and Haithen's new leadership is eager to build a relationship."

"Wait here."

They're left with the second guard and Azure turns and pushes Ocher away from where he's been unsubtly trying to squeeze between him and Ciaran since he walked up. "Knock it off."

"But-"

"I'm tired and you don't get a pass anymore."

"Thank God," Basel mutters. "You two could be incredibly sickening."

"Well, now you have nothing to worry about." He flicks a look at Ciaran, "Probably."

"Azure-" Ocher begins.

"If you say one more word before I get to sleep in a bed. I promise you, Ocher. I will never kiss you again."

It has the intended effect, turning Ocher's expression sullen and he shifts out of sight behind the twins. Not that he would actually keep that promise if it came down to it, but Ocher doesn't need to know that.

"You can come inside," the first guard announces from the doorway.

They're led inside the tower, past a few tastefully decorated halls devoid of anyone else. Their steps sound loudly against the wooden floors and he wonders if there are other people behind any of the doors they pass.

The guard pushes open a door at the end of the hall and they step inside a spacious room taken up almost completely by a circular table in the center.

One lone woman sits on the opposite side of the table and the guard bows to her before leaving and shutting the door behind him.

This must be their royalty, Azure thinks.

She stands and as she comes forward, a ripple of long, black hair trails behind her. Up close, he can see that she's not much older than them. Her lips part and a smile breaks out across her tan face.

"Welcome to Vita. I'm Princess Eulysia."

Azure nods and introduces himself and his companions, but doesn't bow. She's not his princess or anyone to him. Although, he *can* sense the energy in her body, a lot stronger than Ciaran's and he's curious to know if the entire royal family possesses the same abilities as the people from Ustrina.

Perhaps that's *why* they're royalty. It could also be the reason she feels comfortable enough to be left alone with six complete strangers.

"You've come to discuss relations between our two nations," she states and he inclines his head. "We were expecting you a lot sooner considering your history of aggressive expansion."

"That's no longer the type of country we are."

She raises an eyebrow at his words, "Really?"

"Yes," he continues. "Those countries are back to governing themselves. We are here about peaceful relations, not to start another war."

"That's interesting," she murmurs. "We don't communicate with the countries to the West of us much because of the mountains, but last we heard, Haithen had taken over every country bordering the mountains."

"And now they're free."

"Unfortunately, my parents are busy at the moment, but I'm sure they would be more than happy to meet you and learn more about Haithen. I'm only the princess, so any decisions between our two countries that I made would of course be unapproved."

"There's no need to rush."

"How long will you be in Vita?"

"Only until we've reached an agreement or disagreement, whichever."

Eulysia nods, "As I'm sure you no doubt saw, our capital is run very efficiently and everyone knows their role. As long as you don't cause any trouble or do anything to disturb the peace, feel free to stay a while."

"Thank you for your hospitality."

"It's the least we could do since you traveled so far. Shall I arrange for someone to show you all around?"

"Actually, we're all tired. If you could point us to a place we could stay, we'd be happy to take you up on your offer tomorrow."

"Visiting delegates stay somewhere else? No need. Stay with us. The middle floors of this tower are all living quarters, we have more than enough room for all of you."

Azure glances back at Basel for affirmation and he shrugs. That's not a no. "Thank you, if it's no inconvenience we'll stay here."

"Perfect," she steps around him and gestures for them to follow her through the door. "I assume you know what's acceptable or not in someone else's home, but please also restrict yourselves to the guest floor, the first floor, and the dining room on the tenth floor which is where meals are served. If you miss one, you can request something from any of the servants you find on the tenth floor and they will make sure it's brought to you."

They pile into a large elevator and everyone gives her a wide berth as she lists off a few more basic rules before they exit onto the eleventh floor.

This floor is decorated far more lavishly than the bottom floor. Tapestries drape the walls and the carpet underfoot is thick and soft. Fresh flower arrangements line the halls and artisanal statues are set up in various corners typically near plush, silk lined chairs.

Eulysia looks back at them, "Do you have any rooming preferences near each other?"

"Those two twins might want to be together, the rest of us have no preference," Azure answers.

The entire floor must be dedicated to housing guests because they are all given individual suites near each other. His own includes a giant canopy bed draped in shades of dark blue to match the room's interior.

Once the door is locked behind him, he can finally let the exhaustion of such a long journey overtake him. He probably will have to siphon off Ciaran just to last the trip and he's almost starting to regret coming. If not for the other boy's presence, Basel might have been returning to Haithen alone.

They won't stay here too long. He'll find out what he needs to know, hopefully come to some agreement, let Haithen do as they please, and then end his days in peace because no matter how much he missed Ocher, he's not sure that the younger male feels the same or if it's just habit to be close to him. Regardless, Azure won't spend his last days fighting with him.

Ocher really may have grown past him and honestly, it's for the best. There won't be any lingering regrets for either of them this way.

CHAPTER 6: OCHER

The morning after they arrive, Princess Eulysia extends her offer of a guide once more and this time, they accept. Refreshed, they meet on the first floor after breakfast and a tall, pale man by the name of Markus meets them.

Together, the seven of them head back out into the city. Basel is on one side of Azure and Ocher makes sure to take the other side. Azure's emotions leaking into his own mind hasn't happened again. It was only the briefest sliver of want, but it was enough to tell him both what, or who, Azure wanted and that somehow their minds had been linked for just a moment.

He didn't get to use that link against Azure for long before he cut it off. It was still enough time to get what he wanted and send back some of the frustration and confusion that Azure always causes him.

And Azure hadn't liked that one bit.

If he can't be happy, then Azure won't be either. There's no way he's going to let Ciaran take his place. They've been through too much together for him to let a stranger wedge them farther apart.

Ocher can admit that the wedge might have been partly his own fault, that still doesn't mean someone else has the right to make it bigger. He doesn't care what Azure wants. It's not happening while he's around.

Same as yesterday, everyone moves through the streets quietly with only a few giving them more than a fleeting glance. Everyone *seems* content, but their silence strikes him as odd. In the few cities he's been to, the people tend to be livelier. These people seem to want to get to their destination and nothing else, no one stops to greet a friend or smile at a child.

Maybe that silence is why everything is so organized. Every storefront is clean and every front yard is tidy. Vita's capital might be bland, but it's nice enough that he couldn't imagine running from here to live in Haithen. He would vastly prefer this bland country than living in a caravan with no home, or risking the mountains.

Instinctively, he reaches out to intertwine his fingers with Azure's and Azure holds on briefly before realizing what he's done and snatching his hand away with a dirty look in his direction.

Ocher frowns. It was just handholding, he's not even being annoying anymore or 'clingy' as Basel calls it.

Their guide stops near a small cafe and tells them they're free to explore on their own and to be back in time for the official dinner tonight. Before departing, he also reminds them of the same rules Princess Eulysia had explained.

"Ocher, you go with Eren."

"Huh?" He turns to where Azure has dragged Ciaran away and left him with the other three members of their group. "I don't..." He wants to argue, but now it feels like if he does, getting on Azure's bad side is a bigger possibility than before. Previously if he disagreed, he'd just get kissed in response.

"Oh, I'm sorry. I thought that's what you wanted."

Azure knows that's the opposite of what he wants. "Fine."

"Don't sound so excited," Eren mutters.

"I'm sorry."

The four of them wander the town and every resident goes out of their way to avoid them while Eren does his best to get him to talk, but he doesn't want to be nice and keep him happy by responding.

He wants Azure.

Basel links an arm through his and drags him forward away from the twins and he pulls back in annoyance. "Don't touch me, Basel!"

"Oh shut up. I'm taking pity on you unless you want to keep listening to Eren. Although he's not so bad, he's so earnest."

Go away, he thinks.

"Ah that's right. You only care about what Azure wants." Ocher shoots him a look and yanks his arm free. "Don't deny it. It's killing you inside that he won't give you all of his attention and that you're stuck with us."

He hates that Basel knows what he's thinking, especially because he doesn't even like the guy.

"That's what you get for running away and leaving me to deal with him."

Ocher abruptly turns in the opposite direction. He doesn't appreciate the reminder that they've been together for a year without him. He glances over when Basel catches back up to him. Objectively, he's attractive with his hazel eyes and flawless tawny skin, so he can see why Azure could've been interested in him.

"I hear you two broke up because you're an attention seeking brat," Basel begins again conversationally and he's almost as bad as Eren.

"That's not true."

"Which part?"

"That's not why we broke up."

"So you admit you *are* an attention seeking brat?"

"Maybe," Ocher shrugs. "But don't believe his lies. He didn't care."

Basel slides in closer and lowers his voice. "Be honest, what really happened between you two? Azure says you broke up with him out of nowhere and left within a day."

Ocher hesitates, it might have felt abrupt, but it wasn't his choice to leave that soon. He was essentially thrown out even if Azure says otherwise.

"One day I woke up and Azure wasn't there. My first instinct was to reach for him, but he was gone. Then I got up, and he wasn't around. It was odd without him there, without seeing him first thing and basing my life off his plans for the day." He takes a breath. "I didn't know what to do with myself without knowing where he was. I felt weird all day until he finally found me and set everything right. Turns out his help was requested and when he came back, I was annoyed with myself. Then he smoothed everything over the way he does so well."

"So you left because he skipped one day of giving you his attention?" Basel asks in disbelief.

"No!" He snaps. "After that, I realized I was so attached to him that I didn't even know how to be without him. My entire life revolved around him.*That's* when I knew I had to leave and get some time apart."

"Then I don't get it. What's with you now? You should be happy. You've got a new life with new friends, why don't you let him go? Why even come with us? You could have just said no."

Ocher shoots him an irritated look, "It's not that simple."

"It could be. You left him once for an entire year and you seem just fine. For the record, I don't believe for a second that you would have come back on your own."

How could he have? Azure told him to leave and never come back. How could he return after being told that? "I don't know. I might have. I still missed him." Ugh, why is he telling Basel of all people this?

"But it got less over time, right?" Ocher shrugs and Basel huffs in frustration, nudging him aside to look at one of the few colorful displays on the street. "If you were fine being gone for a year, then why does it matter if he's not with you anymore? You left."

"That wasn't my choice."

He waves it away. "Yeah, Azure might have said some things in anger, but you could have fixed it if you wanted to. Instead, you left! Clearly you wanted to be gone more than you wanted to stay together and now a year later, you decide he's not allowed to move on? You don't even have a claim on him anymore!"

"He came to find *me!* I didn't track him down." None of this is his fault, he didn't tell Azure where he was or ask him to come. He did that all on his own!

"If you couldn't even be bothered to seek him out again, what makes you think you have any right to care about who he's with?"

"I don't know, Basel! I just want him okay!"

"You just want him...okay. It doesn't sound like you actually care about him, you just don't want him looking at anyone else. Is that a reason for him to be with you again? Do you even want to be with him yourself?"

"Go away." His face is getting hot and he's starting to feel a headache forming at all Basel's questions. Too many conflicting thoughts for him to think through right now. Azure never made him think this hard.

"Sounds like a no."

Ocher speeds up, leaving Basel to fall back with Eren and Erina. Basel doesn't get to pass judgement on their relationship. He may be Azure's best friend, but Basel is nothing to him and he doesn't have to listen.

He doesn't think about it often, about whether or not he loves Azure. He doesn't know. Azure has never said he loved him either. Was he happy? Yes, happy and coddled with no sense of independence, but he had never noticed it before that day. Well, that's not completely true.

Occasionally, the thought had crossed his mind. However he could never dwell on that or anything that caused him any type of frustration because then Azure would be close to him and handsy until everything was pushed from his mind and he had forgotten what was bothering him in the first place.

Azure controlled almost every aspect of his life and although he didn't like that once he realized it, does that really outweigh everything else? There were a lot of times when he was just happy. He hasn't found that with anyone else since.

Everything was fine as long as he did what Azure wanted and he was too against losing Azure's affections to really fight him on anything. How could anyone actually expect him to give up being in Azure's good graces? He had almost everything he wanted there.

"God Ocher, it's so hot out here," Azure complains, *but he doesn't move. He stays pressed against his side in the warm sand under the sun beaming down on the two of them.*

"You don't have to be out here with me. It was quiet without you."

"I don't have to be, but I know you'd prefer me here with you."

He's not wrong. The view is perfect from the top of this sandy hill and the only thing that makes it better is Azure here with him. If he asks nicely enough, he can probably get Azure to go down into the valley with him.

It still surprises him how little he saw of the entirety of Haithen throughout his first eighteen years and how much he can see now as they travel.

Ocher slides over into Azure's lap and he only puts up the barest resistance. "It's way too hot for this," Azure complains again, and presses his face into his hair anyway, making no attempt to move. He could stay like this forever.

Ocher turns to meet his mouth briefly and smiles. "It's not that hot."

"What are you thinking?"

"That I want you to stay with me forever."

Azure raises an eyebrow and leans back onto his hands, studying him. "You know how this works. That's up to you. I'm right here."

It *was* up to him and he ruined it. Azure would have stayed with him forever if only he hadn't sought more. Now he has less than ever before.

◆ ◆ ◆

They arrive back well in advance of their scheduled time to find that the official dinner has been postponed. The King and Queen left for an emergency issue south of the capital, Eulysia informs them over the tea she's invited them to attend.

The seven of them sit scattered around the sitting room and Ocher tries his best not to let his dislike of the tea show. Why is everything in this country sweet? The sweet and spicy soup he was given before and now this sugary tea.

A housekeeper enters the room with a duster in hand and she freezes at the sight of them, eyes going wide in surprise and something else he can't identify.

"My apol-"

"Do not speak unless you are spoken to," Eulysia's sharp voice cuts across the woman's own. The woman goes rigid. "Well? You've interrupted us now. What do you have to say for yourself?" The woman says nothing and Eulysia tuts. "Now you choose to be silent."

The door opens behind her again and another man steps forward with jerky movements to drag her out by the arm. Ocher barely glances back at them, his eyes are on Azure, so he doesn't miss the sharpening of his gaze on the two of them as the woman is dragged from the room.

"I apologize, she must be new. Most servants here should know better than to interrupt."

"What will happen to her?" Eren questions, ignoring the elbow Erina gives him.

"She'll spend some time below ground and then perhaps she'll have a better recollection of the rules of etiquette in this tower." She looks to Azure. "I'm sure you understand. In your own capital, order has to be enforced as well."

Azure rarely interacts with anyone who keeps his home running. He doesn't know what rules they follow. As if to confirm his thoughts, Azure brings his cup to his lips to take a drink without responding. Instead, he appraises her in silence over the rim of his cup.

"Ocher," he says suddenly. "Try not to wander around here alone too much. I wouldn't want you to break any unspoken rules."

His gaze shifts from Azure to Eulysia's unsmiling face. She gives a short laugh. "Our guests aren't expected to know the rules. That would be inhospitable of us." Eulysia turns from him and then her smile is back. She looks toward Ciaran, "This one, he's not from Haithen, is he?"

"No, we picked him up on the way here. Ciaran volunteered to show us the way."

"How kind of him."

"Yes it was," Basel agrees, standing up to move closer to them. He shoots Azure a warning look and pulls Eulysia's attention to him with an easy smile and a few polite words. Ciaran looks uncomfortable and after what looks like a quick internal debate, he moves to sit with Eren and Erina out of Eulysia's direct line of sight.

Is he the only one that missed something here?

Later that night, after a small dinner that Eulysia declines to attend, he goes searching for answers from Azure. Azure's allocated room is empty and he doesn't have the courage to check Ciaran's room. He asks a passing servant if they've seen Azure and he's relieved to be given directions to a different area of the tower.

Ocher takes the elevator to the second floor and follows the directions to a side door where another servant waves him through and into a long hall. If the hall wasn't so well lit and perfectly maintained, he would be wary of walking alone down an unknown hall alone after Azure's warning.

He comes out into a large changing hall, equipped with baskets and thick towels. The first thing he notices is the humidity of the area, perceivable before he even exits into the hot springs.

Ocher hesitates in the changing hall, unsure if Azure is alone or if his company would even be welcome. There's something worse about being rejected when you're missing clothes.

He's nervous as he strips down, leaving himself in only a towel when he pushes open the door. Azure's gaze locks on him the moment he steps inside and he frowns, saying nothing.

The choice is his.

Ocher steps closer without breaking eye contact and for the first time he notices how tired the other boy looks. Azure's black hair falls around his bare shoulders to pool in the water around him, contrasting against the olive tone of his skin and it's his eyes that really show his exhaustion, dark crescent moons under them that somehow slipped past his attention for the entire time they traveled here.

Even so, Azure is still beautiful and familiar and everything he's come to associate with happiness. Suddenly he's filled with an ache to belong to him again, to know what's bothering him, and to be able to ask.

Love me and only me.

Ocher approaches him slowly and Azure doesn't react as he enters the water and moves forward until he's standing right in front of him.

Azure wrinkles his nose slightly and leans back, sending small ripples of water towards him. Ocher ignores the slight rejection and steps into his space until they're almost chest to chest.

"How did you find me?"

"I asked."

"Maybe I wanted to be alone."

"I don't want you to be away from me." Ocher shifts forward, wrapping his arms around Azure's neck, and pressing close to kiss him. It's the first time he's really initiated something since Azure had found him again and he's relieved Azure doesn't push him away.

Instead he opens his mouth, willing to deepen the kiss for now. No matter what he pretends, Azure loves intimacy. Not a day went by when they didn't engage in something borderline physical.

"I still think you're annoying," Azure murmurs against his lips when he pulls back the barest breadth.

"I know," he answers, dragging him back into a slow, languid kiss. Azure responds in kind, guiding Ocher's legs around his waist, and lifting him easily. Normally, he would have been worried about this going farther, but he doesn't think Azure has forgiven him enough to want sex from him. He won't engage in that type of intimacy when there's no trust between them.

"Let me sleep with you tonight," Ocher whispers into their kiss.

"Why should I?"

"Because I want to." Azure doesn't respond, just kisses him harder and that says everything. He'll allow it, but he won't be nice about it.

CHAPTER 7: AZURE

They spend another two days in Vita, enjoying the country and scoping out reasons people might choose to leave. There's plenty of time to do this because somehow situations keep arising that require the King and Queen's attention, so they have yet to meet.

Answers from the citizens aren't forthcoming either. They've been labeled outsiders and no one makes an effort to speak with them. All interactions are short and to the point if they're buying something or nonexistent if they're not.

There are no signs that the people have been tortured or abused either, giving him a feeling that the danger is far more subtle than he thought. In fact, it probably comes exclusively from the royal family who he has yet to meet in its entirety.

He can sense the power from Eulysia, stronger than Ciaran's, but more diluted than those from Meio. They must have been forced to do some intermixing within the general population of Vita. Eulysia hasn't done anything much yet, probably wary of revealing too much to an outsider, but she's definitely done something to put so much fear in the tower's servants and such obedience from the citizens.

He doesn't want to stay here much longer. They need to find out why no one wants to come back here, leave, and hopefully never come back. Their group of six is also starting to wear on him. He hasn't spent this much time with this many people in years.

Ocher also hasn't been allowed to sleep with him again since that one night, much to the other boy's ire. He wants something for nothing and it doesn't work like that. Ocher can't leave him and still get all the same benefits he enjoyed. He can sleep alone in his own cold bed.

It's easy to keep Ciaran close by flirting. He's inexperienced and blushes easily, but it aggravates Ocher to see, so he can't do it while all three of them are in the same room or Ciaran gets scared off. Still, he's been feeling a little better recently. They find time to spend together and he's able to siphon off small amounts of energy each time, just enough to keep him ahead of his exhaustion.

Ciaran hasn't said much about his country in the time they've been together, but Azure is positive that he knows more than he's letting on. It's odd though, if he thought the capital was dangerous, why would he be so eager to come here?

"Ciaran, you're staring...again."

"Sorry," he apologizes quickly, glancing away. Not that there's anywhere else for him to look. They're sitting right across from each other sharing one of Vita's sweet delicacies, he's directly in Ciaran's line of sight.

"Is there something you want to ask?"

"No, I mean, yes, just who are you?"

"Who...am I?"

"Yes, why are you...*you!*" Ciaran gestures vaguely with red cheeks and Azure huffs in amusement. "You're very..." He mutters something too low for Azure to catch. "And you have a nice smile, your hair is really long and nice too. You have so much confidence and you also take care of Ocher even though he's mean."

Azure laughs, "Don't take him personally. He has some other issues going on."

"He still looks like he wants to kill me most of the time."

"He won't," Azure reassures him. "It would make me mad and he doesn't want that."

Ciaran nods, "Everything else though, I probably didn't explain it very well, did I?"

"It's okay," Azure says, propping his chin up on his hands and gazing back at him. "I understand what you mean."

And he does. Ciaran has a crush on him. That's basically what Ciaran's saying and he hasn't done anything to discourage it. It suits his purposes, but it won't ever go farther.

Ciaran isn't his type.

For all that he's fairly cute and submissive, two things that would usually have him interested, Ciaran seems too soft and trusting. Too easy to break. He's too open and willing, the friendly type, close with everyone. He could never be with someone so quiet and docile, eager to make friends. It's a turn off to someone as inflexible and possessive as he is.

He doesn't think Ciaran could handle it either.

"Let's go, Ciaran."

"Go where?" He glances up in confusion. "You don't want to finish this?"

"Nah, I don't really like sweets. I got it for you."

"Oh," he looks back down at the table. "I'm done too then. I can't finish it on my own."

Azure shakes his head before gesturing at Ciaran to stand. "Come onr then."

They only get a few steps before he feels tentative fingers in his hair. He almost says something, but his tablet vibrates and that's more important. Besides, although he doesn't like other people's hands in his hair, he can drain more of Ciaran's energy through touch, so he'll allow it for a few minutes.

He pulls out his tablet and skips all his unread messages to select Basel's. Unlike Haithen, service in Vita is only in the capital and even here, it's tightly controlled. Without Eulysia's permission, they wouldn't have been able to access the network here either. He checks Basel's message and huffs out a short laugh. *Eulysia's parents are finally able to meet us for dinner. Where are you?? You better not be with that boy, he's gonna lose it.*

Maybe so, Azure thinks, tucking his tablet away, but Ocher has no one to blame except himself. He looks back at the feeling of fingers continuously carding through his hair and raises an eyebrow.

"Sorry, I'd been wanting to touch your hair forever. Why is it so long?"

Azure shrugs, "I like it this way and now I'm used to it."

"I like it too," Ciaran smiles, letting the strands fall through his fingers.

"Good, we should head back. I think we'll finally get to meet the King and Queen, then we can leave. Basel's getting tired from the lack of people willing to entertain him."

Ciaran shifts back a step, face closing off somewhat. "Right."

"Is that face because we might be leaving soon or because they might recognize you?"

"Both."

"You don't want them to know about you? I thought you wanted to meet your family."

"No, I wanted to see the capital and maybe see what the royal family was like if I had the chance. They sent me to the farthest part of Vita, I think it's clear that they don't want me here, who-ever I belong to. I might not even be directly related to them."

You definitely are, Azure thinks. "You were never going to ask about who sent you away?"

"No. It could've been anyone. There are other offshoots of the royal family in control of the outer areas. I don't want to get mixed up in their lives either. After seeing the capital, I'd rather stay in my small town."

"So, you think there's something odd here too?"

"Not odd," Ciaran clarifies. "It's well known that the citizens of Vita are obedient, but no one here seems happy either. They're almost lifeless, yet no one moves away from the capital. I just don't see why people would choose to live here."

"Maybe they don't have a choice." Ciaran looks at him and he shrugs. "They want people kept here so much that they leave giant feral wolves in the only way out to deter people. I don't think it's too much of a stretch to say that maybe they have guards in place to keep people from leaving."

"The wolves are there naturally," Ciaran defends.

"Are they?"

"Maybe...they were bred," Ciaran confesses. "Myrta said never go into the mountains because they were created to tear people apart."

Azure nods, "People are definitely forced to stay here then and they're not happy about it."

"You're not going to say anything about it, are you? Don't say anything," Ciaran pleads. "I still live here!"

"I'm not," Azure reassures him in amusement. "I have four people that I'm somehow responsible for getting back to Haithen. I don't want to find out what they do when challenged either."

"Okay, okay good."

Azure laughs and throws an arm around Ciaran's shoulders to drag him along, "Don't worry. If they figure you out, I'll protect you." Ciaran shoots him a skeptical look through his blush.

"Really I will, they can't do anything with the delegates watching."

"You better…"

"Promise."

◆ ◆ ◆

Back at the tower, he and Ciaran are shown to a sitting room on the eleventh floor where everyone has already gathered. The first thing he sees upon entering the room is the unimpressed look on Eulysia's face directed towards Basel who's doing his best to keep Ocher from cornering him. It's almost guaranteed that Basel did something to provoke him again.

"Azure, get your brat right now before I kill him!" Basel shouts once they're spotted and Ocher immediately whips around to find him.

Azure scoffs, "As if you could."

"Shall we find out?"

"You should keep your people in line," Eulysia interrupts. "I take it that you're the leader of this delegation for a reason, correct? Their behavior would be unacceptable for anyone representing Vita in any official capacity. Is this also what the leadership in Haithen is like?"

Yes, Azure answers internally. Ocher and Basel are both close to him and as such, no one tells them to behave or reprimands them because they don't want to deal with him. Unfortunately for Eulysia, this is exactly how they act back home and no one tries to stop them.

Ocher wouldn't think twice about attacking Basel, no matter where they were if he's annoyed enough and Basel never misses a chance to goad. Time apart hasn't changed that.

Azure sighs. "Come here, Ocher," he orders.

Reluctantly Ocher shuffles over until he's close enough for Azure to grab his arms and drag them around himself. He presses close in the circle of his arms until Ocher has no choice but to look up at him. Azure presses a kiss to his forehead, "I'm not with him."

Ocher flinches. "I don't care if you are or not."

"Mhmm. You liar. Basel said you wanted to tear his head off for saying it."

He glares in the culprit's direction, "Basel is the *liar*."

"Uh huh." Azure turns to Ciaran and gives a half-hearted shrug. "I'm his only friend. I have to be patient sometimes," Azure explains, ignoring the way Ocher's fingers begin digging into his back in anger. They can talk about it later, maybe.

Eulysia stands and points them towards the door, "Well, now that everyone is here, let's have dinner. The meeting is long overdue."

She leads them to the dining hall and takes a seat near the end of the table next to the queen. The queen is a pale skinned woman with green eyes, wearing a silver crown upon her intricately braided locks. At the head of the table is the King, a tall, dark skinned man with brown eyes and a gold crown nestled in his tight black curls.

Both of them stare at their group with a detached curiosity and he understands now where Eulysia gets it from. Azure feels the faintest sensation in his mind and almost against his will, he's bowing to the both of them. Out of the corner of his eye, he sees the rest of his companions do the same.

That's...suspicious. And now he's starting to confirm his thoughts on what the real danger in Vita is.

They take their seats almost robotically and Azure wonders if anyone else realizes what's happening. Probably not since the actions aren't truly against the normal flow of things.

Ocher moves towards the seat a few spots down from his own, then suddenly pulls back to stare at the chair in confusion. He takes another step closer to the chair and shakes his head before abruptly turning and taking the seat next to Azure before Eren can sit.

Azure laughs inside. Subtlety won't work on Ocher's habits. Sitting away from him goes directly against Ocher's instincts. Of course he would shake off that type of interference. Ocher slides his chair over and Azure's not sure if it's from his want to be closer or because he can sense something strange going on.

"I am King Vin. My wife, Euna, and you have already met our daughter Eulysia. I may be the last to say this, but welcome to our country."

"Thank you. We look forward to bringing our two countries closer together," Azure replies.

"Yes. We are quite curious about the recent changes within Haithen. That should be interesting to hear." Azure gives a small smile in acknowledgement. The truth is not something he wants to bring to their attention.

The first courses are served and he sighs as Ocher immediately stakes his claim by picking things off his plate. He's already invading his space, so it's nothing for him to reach over and select what he likes.

He supposes this is his own fault too, more of the lack of boundaries between the two of them that they lived with. In retrospect, no wonder Basel always made snarky comments about their behavior. After a few bites, Azure shifts his plate over. No matter how delicious the appetizer may be, he doesn't eat much these days.

The rest of the courses pass in much the same way. Polite conversation between their two parties that he leaves to Basel. Subtle questions intended to get the truth out in the open without outright asking. Why did Haithen's policies change? How are people doing? Does Vita have a population deficit?

None of the answers matter to him and halfway through the meal Azure finds his face buried in Ocher's hair, inhaling the familiar scent of him as he continues to eat his favorite parts from both their plates.

He's tired. What he wouldn't give to be back in his bed in Haithen right now with Ocher in his arms.

"Azure, you do realize we're representing Haithen, right?" Basel asks loudly to get his attention.

"So?"

"So, we're not at home. Stop letting him do that. This is why he's the way he is."

"How? Perfect?"

"No!" Basel rolls his eyes. "Spoiled rotten."

His eyes open slowly, "What do you want me to do?"

"I don't know? Maybe set some boundaries?"

He wonders how much of this is Basel versus how much he's being impressed upon to say something. "Ocher stop."

"No."

Azure shrugs. "I tried." Ocher doesn't care, and why should he? No one would say anything in Haithen and neither of them really care what Vita thinks.

"At least try to make a good impression," Basel glares at him from across the table.

"*You* make a good impression, you matter more than me anyway."

Ocher looks up, "What's that mean?"

"Don't ask questions while you're eating," Azure says.

Queen Euna looks at them in confusion. "Are you all really the delegation that Haithen chose to send? You're all children, lacking tact and decorum as well."

"I told you they had very little propriety," Eulysia agrees.

"We've only been delegates for about two years," Basel explains. "And there weren't a lot of candidates willing to come here."

"I can't imagine why," Queen Euna responds flatly and exchanges a look with her husband. She turns back to them and her gaze has sharpened.

"Shit," Azure curses softly. He can feel it, the dynamics have just changed. They're no longer seen as equal delegates, but lessers who can be overcome easily. No more subtlety is needed with them.

Queen Euna turns to Basel, "Who is in charge of your country?"

"Azure is," he answers without hesitation.

She raises an eyebrow in surprise, "So you're not mere delegates. The leader of Haithen himself came to visit us. And why is that?"

"Well that's because he-"

Azure cuts in before Basel can unknowingly reveal too much, "I volunteered since we wanted to know more about Vita."

"And when did he take over?" She directs her question to the twins and they give identical head shakes. Her eyes skim over Ciaran and settle on Ocher. "What are things like at Haithen's capitol, do they all obey him?"

"I think I'm doing fine," he answers for Ocher, pulling the other boy up from his seat and towards the door. Ocher knows too many of his secrets to be left alone with them. "We're tired. We'll head to bed early."

Eulysia barely spares him a glance as her attention turns back to Basel who's beginning to look uncomfortable. "How did he take over so easily? I heard nothing about a civil war within your country."

"Basel," he calls sharply, pushing just enough that Basel turns to him. "You told me you were tired too, let's go." The rest can stay. They don't know anything.

"Uh right," Basel pushes back from the table almost clumsily and Azure grabs hold of his arm to tug him out of the room. "What was that about?" He questions once they're enclosed in the elevator.

"I think I see where Ciaran gets his energy from."

"What energy?" Ocher demands to know.

Unthinkingly, he runs a soothing hand down Ocher's back, "It's nothing." He turns to Basel, "Don't be alone with them."

"That bad, huh?"

"You didn't feel anything at dinner?"

"Maybe a little more talkative than usual."

Azure nods, "That's probably about right." They're very good. Leagues above him.

"Azure, what's going on?" Ocher asks, fingers clenching in his shirt and he blinks down, confused as to when Ocher got that close to him.

"Why are you clinging to me?"

Basel snorts, "You were fine with it a minute ago."

"Don't remember." They step out into the hall and Ocher refuses to let go when he tries to shove him towards his own bedroom. "We'll try negotiations in the morning and then I want to leave the day after that."

"You really think we'll reach an agreement on anything?"

"No, and I really don't care. I can say I tried when we get back." He pushes at Ocher, "Are you really not going to let go?"

"I don't feel safe."

"Safe from *what?*"

"I don't know," he shrugs. "Whatever's bothering you. Let me stay in your room."

"If you don't know what there is to be afraid of, how can you be afraid?"

"Azure," he says, slipping into a familiar pleading tone and dragging out the vowels of his name.

"Brat," He nudges Ocher towards his room. "We'll see you in the morning, Basel."

Basel looks at them in amusement, "Uh huh. Have fun."

Frowning, Azure shoves Ocher forward into the room that he's apparently going to be sharing tonight. He really is too weak for him.

"Keep your distance," Azure orders, finally pushing him away and settling on his bed. "I didn't even say you could stay."

"Azure, you don't have to be so mad at me."

"Should I forgive you?"

"Yes."

"That's not gonna happen. Why don't you go cuddle up with Eren?"

"Not Erina?"

Azure shoots him a disparaging look. "You don't like girls."

"Maybe I changed."

"Fine, Erina then."

"Azure." Ocher drags his name out and he can tell what's coming as the other boy pushes away from the door and drops down in front of him.

"Don't."

"Why not?"

"Because I don't want you to."

"You don't want me to do this or you don't want me?"

"I think you should go back to your room."

"I don't want to."

Azure leans back, studying him. "I don't care what you want." Instead of replying, Ocher pushes forward, placing a hand on each of Azure's thighs and he really doesn't care for where this is going. Azure holds out a hand to keep him back. "Before you do this, know this won't change anything. This won't make me forgive you."

"Who says I want to be forgiven?"

He considers Ocher's words for brief moment, "Do whatever you want then." As long as they have an understanding that he doesn't and won't owe Ocher anything.

He sucks in a quiet breath a few seconds later when Ocher's head sinks between his legs and his mouth closes around him. He's missed this closeness, but he doesn't want anyone that isn't Ocher attached to him this way nor does he have the energy or need to find a person for a single night.

His fingers clench into familiar soft dark brown waves and he's only slightly annoyed that after a year, Ocher is still skilled at knowing what he likes. And more than slightly annoyed that Ocher only does this to get what he wants because he knows it'll work.

He'll let Ocher stay the night here, sleep in his bed, slide under him, and have to endure his smugness. Azure's fingers tighten as he nears the end and he does his best to hold back his gasp as Ocher works him to completion.

Ocher looks up at him from his place on his knees with swollen, red lips and Azure can't help reaching for him. Ocher crawls up to straddle his lap and lean over him with a knowing smile. "I really hate you sometimes," Azure tells him.

"No," he replies smugly. "You love me and hate that you do." Ocher surges forward, pushing him backwards onto the bed and connecting their mouths in a warm, open mouthed kiss.

Ocher's not wrong and that infuriates him all the more. His hands cup around Ocher's face to bring him close and this is so familiar. He wants this again, all the time. He never wanted to lose this. He had done everything he could to keep Ocher with him and it only lasted a year.

He's craved the firmness of Ocher's body pressing against him, the intimacy of the two of them alone together, no boundaries between them. All of his affection had been given to Ocher and somehow he was still the one left behind.

His body aches for this, recognizing his other half, and wanting him closer. Azure takes control of the kiss, claiming once again what should always be his and Ocher cedes easily. Ocher's fingers bury themselves in his hair as he forces him onto his back and Azure thinks he wouldn't have any regrets if he spent his last days this way.

At the first knock on his door, Azure wakes out of a dead sleep into the darkness of the room and shoves Ocher off him, ignoring his sleepy outrage as he strides to the door, grabbing his shirt along the way. He cracks the door open and Eulysia stands on the other side, still fully dressed. "I apologize for the late hour," she begins before he can speak. "We understand that we might have been a bit too intrusive with our questions earlier and we apologize for that as well."

"It's fine. I understand curiosity." She nods, but makes no move to leave. "Is there anything else?"

"Yes, my parents would like to speak with you again."

"Right *now?*" He glances back to where Ocher's sluggishly dragging himself out of the bed. "It can't wait until morning?"

"We want to clear up any misunderstandings. You don't have to wake everyone up, just you will be enough."

"And me," Ocher interjects, latching onto him.

Eulyisa raises an eyebrow, "*This* is how you choose to instill obedience? Bad behavior should not be rewarded."

"I'm not his parent."

"Aren't we all somewhat like parents to our subjects?" She counters. "Bring him if you must."

This time, they take the elevator a few floors up and exit into a hallway even more lavishly decorated than the guest floor. There are fewer doors on this floor and Eulysia leads them through an arch in the back that ends in a room encased by a glass ceiling.

She presents the two of them and takes a seat next to her parents, dimly illuminated by only the moon and a few hanging lanterns.

King Vin speaks first. "I apologize again for our aggressiveness at dinner. We only wanted to know what kind of threat Haithen posed to Vita. Your country doesn't have the best reputation and now you're here, wandering through our country. It is understandable that we would be concerned."

"Of course," Azure agrees. "But, I don't see why this couldn't have waited until morning."

"It seems we neglected to consider your exhaustion in our haste to make things right. Please give us a few more minutes of your time. We won't take long."

Azure doesn't think they *neglected* it at all. In fact, he's pretty sure they were well aware of the time and woke them up regardless. What does their comfort matter against what the regents of this country want?

"We were eventually going to reach out to Haithen ourselves, if only to prevent any hostile encroachment, however it seems like leadership changed before we had to."

"And now?"

"Now, we're still curious about Haithen and you've saved us the trouble by coming to us, so thank you." Azure remains silent, waiting to see how this will play out. "First, you've seen our country and our ways, now it only makes sense that we should know more about Haithen before coming to any agreement."

"What do you want to know?"

"Why did leadership change?"

"The people were tired of being oppressed, so some of them fought back. They went directly after our previous leader and everyone else kind of fell in line after that."

Queen Euna raises an eyebrow, "An unusually peaceful takeover."

"There were a few lives lost," Azure says. "They weren't important. Haithen came out better for it."

"And how did you, barely out of youth, come to be in charge of an entire country?"

"I helped fight back and it was unanimous."

She nods slowly, then gestures at Ocher, "Who is he?"

"Mine."

"Pardon?"

"You asked who he was and I told you, he's mine."

Queen Euna smiles faintly and trades a look with her husband. The two of them turn to face him and he feels the faintest touch to his mind, testing him. He can stop them if need be, but he has no protections in his mind nor does he have the skill to try the same thing against them.

He does nothing, waiting to see what they want. Their parallel touch glides over his mind and finally settles, confirming what he already suspected. The royal family controls their population through the energy of their minds, an ability neither Ustrina nor Meio practiced. His only practice is the clumsy emotional manipulation he sometimes used when Ocher got particularly agitated.

The touch grows slightly heavier and he finds himself on his knees in front of them while Ocher looks on in surprise. It'll be easier to let them do this without fighting back. Once he's out of their presence, he can leave without suspicion. Besides, there's a chance that if he fights back, they might respond with aggression that he's too weak to counter right now.

"When you return to Haithen," King Vin begins. "You will tell them that you are making an alliance with Vita. We will send some of our people to stay with you and join your advisors. In exchange, two of your highest ranking officials will return to Vita to meet with us."

Their plan to infiltrate and take over Haithen isn't amicable at all. No advisor in Haithen will agree to this, so Azure assumes they're counting on him to overrule as leader and force Vita's will on them. He may be in charge of Haithen, but any attempt to take power from the officials will start a rebellion, futile or not.

Nonetheless, he lets them guide his head into a nod as they cement their desires into his mind. This is almost over.

Or it would be if he had remembered that Ocher is his own type of protective. "Azure, why are you agreeing to this? We don't owe them anything."

He doesn't respond. That would be revealing that they don't have complete control over him.

"*Azure,*" Ocher grabs onto his arm and pulls. "Let's go. I'm tired. You can talk about it with Basel in the morning." Suddenly, he freezes, fingers turning stiff around his arm. Shit.

Eulysia has her gaze on Ocher, no doubt reveling in the opportunity to make him behave as she wants. Whereas he hadn't bothered to fight back, Ocher doesn't have that same sense of self-preservation.

He doesn't know what Eulysia's trying to force him to do but Ocher shakes with the effort of resisting and he can't even say anything.

She frowns, "He's resisting me."

"How is that?" Queen Euna wonders. She looks at Ocher, "Unless he's from Meio and has some amount of natural protection."

"Then it would make a lot more sense why the leader of Haithen would let him act however he pleases," Eulyisa agrees. She turns towards her mother, "We can't allow him to go back and ruin our plan. Perhaps, we should do Haithen a favor and rid them of their problem."

"I agree. He won't be missed, keep him here and we'll have this one make up some lie to tell the others."

Ocher steps back, shaking off more of her control and Eulysia turns to him under the watchful gazes of her parents. Ocher looks to him, warring internally about whether to run or stay. Even under the threat of death, leaving him goes against everything he feels.

When Ocher makes a decision and grabs his arm again, Azure almost wishes Ocher had a little more distance when it comes to him. Eulysia doesn't delay, she throws a mental grip onto Ocher so strong that Azure can feel it through the tight gates of their bond.

Like before, Ocher fights back, refusing her control and this time she doesn't ease up. She presses harder and Azure can see this going badly because Ocher won't stop resisting.

His face is beginning to redden from the strain when he decides enough is enough. Azure throws off Queen Euna's control and cuts through Eulysia's hold on him right as Ocher collapses. Azure reaches out to catch him, "You okay?"

"No," he groans. "My head."

Ocher has a bit of his power inside him helping him resist, but that won't stop his mind from breaking if she keeps pushing.

Azure turns to the three regents of Vita and takes a breath. All three look at him in shock and this won't end well for anyone from Haithen if they get control of him. Rather than waiting for them to recover from their surprise, he gives thanks that he siphoned for Ciaran earlier today and uses the last bit of his energy, boosted by his amplified abilities, to knock them out.

It's messy, unfocused, and the effort leaves him staggering, but it does the job. Eulysia drops to the ground and the other two slump over in their seats. He's too weak for the effects to last long, so they have to move fast.

He tightens his grip on Ocher, who's unconscious now, and hauls him to the elevator, leaning him against the door once they reach their floor. Azure enters his own room and grabs his bag before pushing open each of the twin's doors and telling them to get up.

Azure pulls Basel, the only other person here he cares about, from his bed. "We're leaving right now. Get up or I'm leaving you. Get the keys."

"What happened?"

"Just move."

Without waiting for a response, he moves back to the elevator and lifts Ocher's arm around his shoulders. Silently, Basel comes up to take his other arm and together the five of them cram into the elevator.

It's a tense ride down and everyone is wise enough not to bother him with questions. The guards at the front door let them pass without much more than a confused look, even though it's after midnight. Their job is to keep people out, not in.

The streets are silent and empty, allowing them to move quickly towards the outskirts. They have a long walk to the city's barricade, but once they reach their vehicle, they can put distance between themselves and the capital much faster.

Fast paced footsteps sound behind them once they reach the street leading out of the city and Azure tenses. He thought they had more time than that.

Ciaran comes running towards them and Azure relaxes. He's no threat. "Don't leave me!" Ciaran takes in the sight of them, half dressed and carrying Ocher. "Are you running away? What happened?"

"Either leave or stay," Azure replies curtly. They still have several miles to go.

Ciaran looks at the others and they shrug, confused as well. "I'll come," he says, falling into step with them.

Good, Azure thinks. He's running on empty again. They can drop Ciaran off at his village before leaving and he can siphon a bit more of his energy on the way. At least, he finally knows what happened to the offshoot of his people who left Meio and came East. He never would have thought they would choose the manipulation of human energy as their path. Ustrina and Meio stayed far from that.

It's still dark when they pass through the barricade and he and Basel lift Ocher into the back of the truck. He hasn't woken up again and Azure presses a brief hand to his face to ensure he's physically okay before climbing into the passenger seat.

The barricade falls behind them as Basel gases it, sensing how important it is that they get away. They drive nonstop, skipping food and any type of break. He doesn't know whether King Vin will pursue them or find it to be too much effort and he doesn't want to know. For once in his life, he just wants to be safe in Haithen.

Hours later, their first stop is Ciaran's town. They drop off a drained Ciaran to Myrta and Azure refuses to let them stay here and take a break despite their protests. It's not worth the risk. They get a few minutes to stretch, then he demands everyone back inside. He hopes he never sees this country again.

Basel is understanding without knowing what's going on. He starts the truck up with no complaints, but he does insist on switching seats so he can rest. Azure agrees. He should be able to get far enough into the mountain before he also has to sleep and recover.

They head up the mountain, tensing in anticipation of any attack as he drives higher up on undefined paths. The sun drops below the horizon, bringing full darkness and Azure sighs as he feels Basel's glare on him. He won't like what happens next either.

Azure slows the vehicle to a stop and switches to park. "We're going to have to stop. I'm too tired to keep driving in the dark."

"Are you crazy?" Basel near shouts. "There are wild animals out here!"

"Basel, this truck is armored. They weren't able to get through before and they won't be able to now. I think we've gone far enough that we should be safe if Vita had tried to pursue us. Unless you want to drive, we don't have another option."

"I can barely keep my eyes open either, you know it'd be dangerous if I got behind the wheel."

"Then, we'll be fine," Azure says before opening his door.

"Where are you going?" Basel asks in alarm.

"To give us some cover." He had parked the truck next to a snowdrift to make it easy for him to climb into the back, then bring the piles of snow down around them, camouflaging them and shrouding the inside of the truck in darkness.

Basel lifts his tablet to give them some light, "Burying us under snow was your plan?"

"They can't see us, we can't see them. Now everyone can sleep without worry." He turns away from them and focuses on Ocher who's finally stirring awake. "You okay?"

"Why is it so dark and cold?"

"We're back in the mountains." He reaches for one of the blankets in the back and wraps it around Ocher, cradling him in his arms.

"You're coddling him again," Basel comments. "I guess he was right, you wouldn't care if he was clingy."

Azure gently cards his hand through Ocher's hair as he feels him growing heavy with sleep again, "Why would I mind? I did nothing to discourage him."

"You two really deserve each other."

"I thought so too at one point," he says, stretching out in the small space, but now he's not so sure.

◆ ◆ ◆

"Azure, wake up." A hand jostles him roughly, smacking him across the face with a not insignificant amount of force. "It's morning, it's cold, and I'm ready to go."

He shifts Ocher off him, sits up, and almost loses his balance from an unexpected bout of dizziness. This is bad, he thinks. Not unexpected, but he feels worse than before he siphoned off Ciaran. Azure lays back down and pushes the snow away from them to clear the path for Basel to continue driving. Even that bit of exertion leaves him sweating. He needs food and his bed and maybe to avoid using his power for the rest of his life. He doesn't want to die in the back of a truck.

"Am I dumping them back in their town?" Basel shouts back to him.

"Just take me home, we can put them on a train later."

He spends most of the ride back lethargic and weak, too exhausted to do more than answer an occasional question.

At one point, he feels Ocher's fingers wandering across him and a mouth pressing gently against his own. All he can muster is a groan of protest that Ocher easily ignores.

He doesn't have the strength to push Ocher off, and if he did, he's not sure that he would. He's missed him, almost too much. It feels right when he's nearby, when he presses close and Azure can feel the force of their bond between them.

It makes everything better and he suspects Ocher knows that his feelings run deeper than he says. Ocher has too much power over him and it's worse that he knows it.

CHAPTER 8: OCHER

What the hell happened in Vita? And what did they do to him? He barely remembers driving back to Haithen and nothing about leaving the country. He woke up in the back of the truck the first time and Azure's arms were around him. Even now, his head still feels a little fuzzy.

This time, he'd woken up in his own bedroom back in the home he used to share with Azure and nothing inside his room has changed. Everything has been left in the same place as if he'd only stepped out for a moment.

He didn't expect to be back here so soon.

It's morning when he steps outside onto the perfectly manicured lawn. It's still so comforting to him after an entire year away. He's surprised to see Sara outside with the twins, had she moved in once he left or is she visiting? She hasn't changed either, wearing another one of her frilly dresses in sky blue this time.

"Ocher!" She shouts once she catches sight of him. Sara runs over, red hair flying behind her, and hugs him. "How are you feeling? Azure said you had an accident."

"I feel better than before. You've seen him?"

She frowns, "I think he wasn't feeling well either."

"Oh. He must still be mad at me, he wouldn't let me near him, so I can't check on him."

"Yeah," Sara nods with sympathy in her brown eyes. "He doesn't forgive easily, not even you."

Her words are true, yet they still hurt. He thought that maybe after that night Azure would be more open to forgiving him, especially the way Azure had held him in the truck. But apparently he meant what he said, that nothing between them would change. He feels overwhelming sadness at the thought. He doesn't know how to make Azure forgive him.

Eren and Erina approach them and the atmosphere turns cooler at their arrival. Sara laughs it off, not one to let any awkwardness stand. She loops an arm through each of theirs, ignoring their less friendly gazes, and pulls the two of them to a table. Ocher follows after them, he has nothing else to do.

He takes a seat and almost immediately a worker brings him food, setting a raspberry tart and glass of milk in front of him. His mouth waters, he missed these. Azure had instructed the cooks to learn different raspberry dishes to suit his tastes and he wonders if they immediately set to preparing his favorites when they saw he was back or if Azure had something to do with it.

The first bite is tart on his tongue and it's just as delicious as he remembers.

"How did they know you like raspberries?"

He turns to Eren, "What?"

Eren gestures at their matching plates, "No one asked us what we wanted, they just brought what *you* liked right away. How did they know your favorite food is raspberries?"

Ocher shrugs, "Azure told them."

"It's also weird that I asked someone where you were and they said they couldn't tell me where your bedroom is. Not that they didn't *know*, they just wouldn't tell me. All the people who work here said the same. Do you have your own personal bedroom here?"

"Azure assigned me a room like he did everyone." He takes another bite, "Sara, where's your room?"

She looks at him slyly, "Near yours." Ocher shoots her a withering look. She can be as bad as Basel when she wants to be.

"Have you been here before?" Erina picks up the questioning.

"Yeah."

"When? After you left your fishing town?"

Sara blinks at him in surprise and he ignores her. "Yes, between then and moving to your town."

"Wow, you get around quite a lot," Sara comments idly. "Fishing town, I know you did more than visit Azure here. Then you moved again, can't keep you in one place."

The twins are looking at him in confusion, probably trying to piece together the timeline, and he doesn't want to be around when they figure out it doesn't make sense. Or rather when Sara calls him out, she's way more loyal to Azure than she'll ever be to him.

Ocher drops his fork onto his empty plate and stands, "I'm gonna go check on Azure."

"Don't bother," an unwelcome voice says behind and he turns to face Basel. "He won't see you. Also, there's a meeting about what happened in Vita, let's go."

He hates meetings, but whenever he's here, he's required to go unless Azure lets him off and since Azure is refusing to show himself, he doesn't have a choice.

A quick goodbye to the twin's confused faces and he follows Basel into the meeting room. They take seats on opposite sides of the noticeably empty head chair and Kronos glances from him to the chair in distaste. The man was never fond of him.

The most surprising thing is that Dominicus is in the room as well. Azure had rarely ever let Dominicus be in a single meeting despite being one of the head captains, that's one thing that's changed.

Dominicus smiles at him and it's the same wide, warm smile he grew up with. Inadvertently, he finds himself giving a small smile back. Dominicus is the only person that might even come close to knowing him as well as Azure does.

His chair jostles from a sharp kick and Basel glares with warning when their eyes meet. Ocher glares back, they only smiled at each other. It's not like he's breaking one of Azure's strict rules about contact with Dominicus. If they even matter anymore.

Basel clears his throat to grab the room's attention, "Azure won't be joining us today. He's still recovering from the trip." Basel goes on to give a report on Vita and their subsequent escape in the middle of the night while he remains silent as usual. He never has much to contribute and it's pointless for him to sit through the meetings, but sometimes sacrifices have to be made.

After Basel's report, they eventually come to the decision to attack preemptively and Ocher doesn't consider it a matter that concerns him. He's not a soldier anymore. He doesn't care what they decide. Although he knows Azure won't like their decision.

Dominicus catches him on his way out the door once they break and sweeps him into a hug. It's his second hug of the day and he has the brief thought of when did people get so affectionate. "What are you doing here?"

"When there might be a war, I need to know about it. I *am* a captain. How have you been? I heard you left for a while."

"Yeah, we had a disagreement." He leaves the answer intentionally vague. Dominicus doesn't know too much about his relationship with Azure and he doesn't want to start confiding in him now.

Sensing his reticence, Dominicus changes the subject, "Hey, you probably haven't been out on the field in a while. Want to spar?

It'll keep your mind off things."

Ocher hesitates. If he goes, he can't tell Azure. Breaking Azure's rules will really screw things up if he finds out. Then again, Azure won't even face him, so what does it matter, he thinks spitefully. "Okay."

Dominicus grins and throws an arm around his shoulders, "It'll be fine, you look like you need to let off some steam anyway."

Does he? Maybe he feels a bit more on edge than usual, but he figured that was a result of what happened in Vita and being back here.

Dominicus guides them a little ways off to an open clearing with a wide dirt circle drawn around it. "Like it?"

"What is this?"

"Outside training ground," Dominicus answers. "You wouldn't know about it since you've been gone so long and before that, you had already quit being a soldier."

Ocher grimaces. None of them would have chosen that life if they had a choice, he was just fortunate enough that he didn't need to stick around once it was no longer required. "I'm here now."

"Yeah, let's see if you still have anything left." Dominicus lunges and he barely manages to avoid the unexpected attack. "Are you *pouting?*" Dominicus laughs. "When the hell did you pick *that* up?"

Ocher flushes, rearranging his face into hostile neutrality. It's not his fault that he's grown out of hiding his every emotion. Azure didn't like it. Dominicus comes at him again and this time he's ready, blocking easily.

They continue this way, switching between the offensive and defensive to land attacks, lacking the strength to actually injure. Dominicus is right, it does help keep his thoughts at bay.

Sparring requires his full concentration and he easily slips into the familiar pattern of exchanging strikes. It's relaxing in such a simple way.

By the time Dominicus pulls back and calls for a break, he's sweaty and his limbs are loose from the exertion. He feels great.

Dominicus taps the ground beside him and Ocher drops down next to him. "So, where have you been?"

"I went to another town, got a job on a farm, and I've been living there."

Ocher catches the look of disbelief Dominicus sends him in his peripheral vision. "You would leave *here* where you have everything you want without having to work?"

"I wanted independence, that wasn't here."

"You would leave *him* for an entire year?"

Ocher frowns, plucking a few strands of grass and rubbing them between his fingers. It wasn't that bad, he did find the independence he wanted. "Azure wasn't happy when he found out I was leaving. I don't know if I would have been welcome even if I had come back sooner."

"Why are you back now?"

"Do we have to talk about this?"

"Alright." Dominicus scoots closer and Ocher feels the extra heat from their sparring still radiating off him. "What are you going to do now?"

He shrugs, "I don't know." His story is falling apart with Eren and Erina and he doesn't know if he wants to return home with them. He had thought Azure might have been willing to forgive him, but now the other boy won't even see him. He's sad and a little lost.

"Ah, don't make that face. You'll make me cry. You're so expressive now. Do you shout now too?"

"Sometimes." And he probably does a lot more things that should embarrass him, but don't. He's learned that being direct in his wants can sometimes be the best way.

Dominicus laughs again. "I can't believe it. You really have changed."

Ocher shrugs and feels fingers tuck a few loose pieces of his hair behind his ear and he freezes at the intimate touch, eyes darting up from the ground to meet Dominicus's intense stare.

He doesn't know what to do and Dominicus takes his lack of response as permission. He leans in and Ocher leans back, sucking in a sharp breath.

Dominicus pulls back to study him for a moment, "You know I've always liked you, Ocher."

That's news to him. "You never said anything before."

He smiles, "You weren't exactly the most open person and I didn't want to scare you off."

"Oh." What is he supposed to do with that? Act on it? "Azure would lose it if he found out."

"Isn't he terrible to you anyway? Haven't you been broken up for a year now?"

Did they? It didn't feel like it the last night they were in Azure's room back in Vita. But he can't say if they did or didn't. He doesn't know what it is that Azure wants from him, they never talk about anything. They only shout once they've pressed each other's buttons. His head is starting to hurt.

"You're really going to let him keep me from ever getting to kiss you?" Dominicus is his friend, but Azure would not forgive this and suddenly he understands more than ever why Azure set those rules because part of him isn't against giving Dominicus what he wants.

"I've talked to Basel about you and him," Dominicus says. "He told me that you two bring out the worst in each other."

Basel? Ocher frowns. "Don't talk to him about us. I hate him."

Dominicus grins with amusement. "For the same reason that Azure hates me?"

"Kind of," he admits.

Dominicus looks at him with fondness, all warm brown eyes and a soft smile. This time when he leans in, Ocher hesitates. He doesn't lean back and Dominicus kisses him.

He feels Dominicus smile against his lips as a hand slips into his hair, tugging lightly. Ocher kisses him back and Dominicus is so much gentler with him, while Azure always kissed to control.

Ocher pulls Dominicus in closer, feeling his free hand come to rest on his waist and already, he can feel the slight burn in his eyes signaling what's about to come. Instead of pulling away, he kisses harder and lets Dominicus press them together.

He's already ruined everything, why stop now?

CHAPTER 9: AZURE

Azure wakes up with the sensation of guilt and regret weighing him down, he only has a brief moment to think about the source before everything else catches back up to him. He still feels drained and exhausted after sleeping nearly sixteen hours straight. His body won't last much longer.

"About time you woke up." Azure sits up to see Basel stretched out on the edge of his bed. "We had to meet without you."

"And? Let's just let them do what they want is what I hope they decided on."

Basel laughs sarcastically. "Are you kidding me? It was fine while we didn't know, but now we know they're hostile and have ideas about taking over Haithen. They voted to attack in full force. If you didn't want this result, maybe you should've given me a better story about what happened."

Azure pulls the blanket over his head, "Do they ever *stop?*"

"You seriously want to let them control people like that? You said they were taking your free will!"

"Look, they're not hurting anybody from Haithen. What they do to their own citizens is their business. The ones who don't like it have already left."

"Unfortunately Vita is on Haithen's radar now and they're not going to let it go. Don't worry," Basel comforts. "You might be dead by then anyway."

Azure glares. He was doing bad enough without the reminder of his impending death.

There's a knock on the door and Savanta enters. Azure immediately perks up. "Savanta! You've come to take care of me?"

"Not quite," she answers, taking a seat on his other side. "Sara is finishing school soon and she wants to travel. As the highly paid leader of Haithen, she came to ask you for money."

Azure sinks back into his pillows. "Bold, isn't she?"

Savanta shrugs, "You've always spoiled her, it's your own fault. I just came by to see how you were doing." She pauses. "You look pretty bad."

"Well, we have had a rough forty eight hours."

"Hungry?"

"Not really."

"You should eat though," Basel says. "It might help."

"If you two stay with me."

"Fine," Savanta agrees and Basel reaches over to grab a covered tray off his table, then settles down next to him.

The tray of lukewarm food is placed in his lap and Azure relaxes, sandwiched between the two people who know him the best in the world.

Ocher appears at the door to his library that evening, pushing open the door and entering before he can say anything. He couldn't avoid Ocher forever. He's worrying his bottom lip and

Azure's eyes narrow, something's wrong and it could be any number of things.

"Where have you been all day?"

Ocher ignores his question and takes a seat in a nearby armchair, hugging his legs to his chest. "What happened in Vita?"

"They're like me and probably controlling the population mentally."

"Like you do to me sometimes?"

"No. I don't force you into doing things against your will."

"You might not force me, but you have ways of making me do what you want anyway."

"It's not forcing if you have a choice. You just might not appreciate what happens after if you don't. Sometimes, it takes some pressure with you. But, hey, you left, so apparently it's not much of a problem."

Ocher looks at him, "How long are you going to hold that against me?"

"Forever."

"Then why should I bother staying here?"

Azure shrugs, "You're choosing to stay here. I'm not *forcing* you. Leave if you want." He stands from his chair and heads for the door, "Your strays can stay here until you leave if that's what you want." Azure steps out, shutting the door behind him. Ocher can make all the decisions he wants.

He heads straight to his bedroom and slips into the large tub, already filled and waiting for him. As the apple scented steam wafts up, Azure grimaces. This is Ocher's favorite bath scent, not his. They must have put it back when he returned.

Despite that, it's still good to be back home. Though he can also appreciate that bathing room back in Vita. If he was going to be around longer, he might have considered having one built here.

As it stands, he'll enjoy what he has in the time he has left.

Now that he knows where the people who split from Meio went, he's curious to know if they founded Vita or if they took over. The emigration from Vita makes a whole lot more sense after visiting.

The people leaving probably didn't comprehend the full extent of what was happening there or what their royalty was capable of. The citizens just know something is wrong and want to escape.

Vita isn't much smaller than Haithen, so to keep the entire country under control, there are probably branches of the main family set up in different areas of the country to keep all the citizens obedient. It would be too much and too far for the main family to cover everyone, making him wonder just how many enchanters there are living in Vita.

Even if he had the skill to control people that way, he wouldn't. He has no desire for that type of absolute power. He barely wants the control he has over Haithen now. Basel handles most of the politics anyway, his presence is only there as a threat.

For them to subjugate an entire country's population by mental force is nothing short of greed and abuse of their power for no other reason than because they can. It's already been proven twice in Haithen that it's unnecessary to go that far to take over.

Azure sinks below the water, and lets his concern about Vita float away. It's not *his* problem. He's not responsible for what others choose to do with their abilities and he's the last person that should be talking about right and wrong.

He hasn't been innocent since he was a child and he wouldn't change anything if he could.

When he gets out of the tub and returns to his room, Ocher is there shoving all his pillows off the bed to his annoyance. Ocher throws one of the pillows at him the moment he catches sight of Azure, "Why are there so *many* damn pillows?"

"Leave my pillows alone, they belong in my bed more than you do." Ocher goes stiff at his words and he takes the opportunity to toss them back onto the bed. He makes a sound of frustration that Azure ignores and settles into bed instead. "What the hell is wrong with you? You know I like pillows and you've slept in here enough times to know they're not moving."

Azure has a feeling that he knows part of what Ocher's problem is and it's not good. There's a high chance that Eulysia's forceful intrusion into his mind caused some damage. Ocher's emotionally stable enough on most days without any extra intervention, but with all the added stress he seems to be under since they got back plus the effects of fighting off Eulysia's intrusion, it's not a good combination.

"You don't need this many, I'm here!"

Azure blinks over at him, "You have a bedroom down the hall if it bothers you so much."

Ocher screams in frustration and hits him in the head with a pillow. Enough of that. Azure grabs him by the arm and yanks him forward to pin down. He barely puts up a fight, so this must be what he wanted all along.

He presses a hand against Ocher's forehead and the other boy goes comatose the next second. He's gotten better, unfortunately, Ocher has not. His mind is a mess, more knots than he's ever had before. Is this from the year they spent apart or is this from recent events? He wishes he knew, but everything going on with Ocher is a mystery to him now, something he never would have allowed before.

It's annoying, but he can calm him down for a while, maybe even long enough to get the truth from him. Azure presses further into his mind, gently attempting to smooth out the worst parts. If he could just...Ocher shoves him away abruptly.

Azure pulls back in surprise, that's new. Maybe Eulysia did more damage than he thought. Ocher never would have broken free before.

"Whatever you're always doing to me, stop." Ocher looks furious and more than that, distrusting.

"Fine, fine." He shifts away, lowering his voice. "Just trying to help you calm down."

"Stop! Stop *managing* me."

"What are you talking about?"

"You!" He sits up, putting more distance between them. "You were *always* managing me, I told you!"

"Well what was I supposed to do, let you go crazy?"

"No! But you were always making things happy all the time, forcing me to relax anytime I started to feel even a little upset."

"And? What's wrong with that?"

"Because I can't function! This is why I can't deal with things! You were constantly there, smoothing everything over. You control everything, that's why I left in the first place!"

He's not wrong about the nature of their relationship. Ocher's submissiveness and willingness to let him be the dominant one in their relationship without complaint is part of the reason why they worked so well. "That year doesn't seem to have done much."

Ocher attacks and he really doesn't have the energy for this. Instead of fighting back, he easily knocks Ocher's arms aside and presses two fingers to his head, dropping him instantly. Azure shoves his unconscious body aside and gets up.

At least that still works, he thinks. Ocher is giving him too much trouble, should have left him on that farm. He doesn't want to look at this stranger anymore, not the relaxed lines of his face or the soft, kissable shape of his full mouth.

Azure looks away. He's not giving in to any of that.

He ends up in the private kitchen, standing in front of the refrigerator and debating on who he needs to fire for training the workers in this place. He doesn't have many favorite foods himself, but this is ridiculous. Within two days of returning, the fridge has been filled with all of Ocher's preferred snacks and food. Who told them to do that? He hasn't given them any indication that Ocher should be welcomed back.

Sighing, he grabs a cup of milk and a cold slice of pie to eat. The pie isn't even half way finished before he's interrupted.

"Where is he?" Erina stands in the doorway with her brother a half step behind her.

Can't he have peace in his own home? "He's down, probably for the rest of the night."

"Down?" She frowns. "What did you do to him?"

"Wouldn't you like to know."

"Where is his room?"

Azure taps his fork against the plate impatiently. "If he wanted you to know where his room was, he would have told you."

"You would tell us if you weren't so threatened by us."

"I am not threatened by either of you. I let you stay here because you're his friends. Other than that, you're of no concern to me. Now, you're bothering me, so get out."

Threatened by them? Ha, maybe if Ocher had shown the slightest inclination for either of them. As it is, they're nobody and he has no reason to care what they do. Besides, they can't threaten what doesn't exist and he and Ocher no longer have anything.

He hopes his death destroys Ocher inside, makes him unable to be with anyone else. If he can't have a happy ending, Ocher doesn't deserve one either.

His door is cracked open when he returns to his bedroom, which means he'll be sleeping alone tonight. Azure steps inside, only to freeze at the sight in front of him.

Those two unwelcome nuisances are in *his* bedroom, crouched near *his* bed and desperately trying to wake Ocher up. They've crossed a line.

Azure strides forward and yanks Eren back by his neck, throwing him into the opposite wall hard enough to shake the paintings loose. He turns to Erina and she's already scrabbling backwards, hurrying to her brother's side.

"Azure?" Ocher's semi-conscious voice calls to him.

"I'm here." He climbs onto the bed and presses him back into the pillows, running a hand through his hair until Ocher drifts back off. Azure turns and sends the twins a vicious glare, "Get out."

He watches as Erina helps her limping brother to his feet and to the door. Neither of them look back at him in their haste for the exit.

Azure slides in next to him under the blankets and lets Ocher instinctively curl into him.

His stupid smitten friends, he'd kick them out if he wasn't sure Ocher would protest. He might still be mad at Ocher, that doesn't mean he's ready for him to leave again. Ocher should be here with him until the very end.

CHAPTER 10: OCHER

As much as he hates it, it's been a year since he's last been around Azure this much and he can't help wanting to stay close. He's been feeling mostly okay since he recovered from whatever happened to him in Vita, except the tenuous relationship he shares with Azure has been stressing him and the thing with Dominicus didn't help.

What was he thinking? How could he be stupid enough to give in when the entire reason he hasn't left yet is because he wants Azure to love him again? Azure will hate him even more *because* it was Dominicus.

He'd woken up this morning tucked in Azure's arms and he'd wanted to stay there, but Azure wouldn't wake up for hours and he also wasn't sure how to face him right then after yesterday's outburst. He just *knows* that put a bigger wedge between them.

Now, he's braced to apologize and hope that Azure doesn't throw his apology back in his face. Azure demands words, but he makes his decisions based on actions.

It's nearing noon when he figures Azure is awake enough and he gathers the courage to seek him out. He finds Azure near the lake in the private land behind the palace, slowly pulling the water back and forth in gentle waves. Azure once told him that it was calming for him when he has a lot on his mind. It's been a while since Ocher's visited him out here and he doubts it would go the same way as last time.

Azure is in one of his rare affectionate moods and has dragged him out to the lake for reasons known only to him. Ocher wiggles his fingers in Azure's tight grip and he immediately lets go which isn't what he wanted. He just wanted Azure to tell him why they were coming out here.

Before he can protest too much, Azure's yanking him down into his lap. "Don't complain."

"I wasn't!" He was definitely about to.

"I know you." Azure circles arms around his waist and settles him on the ground between his legs, so that their legs dip into the water. "If I'm touching you and move away suddenly, you always *complain. Loudly. Until I come back."*

"Well, stop leaving then," Ocher mutters back sullenly.

Azure presses a kiss behind his ear, then follows up with another to his mouth. "Of course."

"Good," Ocher settles back against his chest, watching as Azure begins to shape the water with a wave of his hand.

At his command, the water dances through the air, splitting and joining in intricate, three dimensional shapes. Behind him, he can feel Azure relaxing and privately, he's pleased that Azure cares enough to share something he might normally do on his own with him.

Now that they have no goals anymore, or maybe because he'd professed his unwavering loyalty to Azure, he's nowhere near as mean as he was before.

He startles at the splash of cold water that pours over him, drenching him instantly. That was definitely on purpose. Ocher turns, "What the hell, Azure? I'm soaked!"

Azure shrugs, meeting his gaze evenly. "Then take them off."

"You would like that, wouldn't you?"

"I would," he agrees easily.

Ocher turns in his lap with a shake of his head and peels his wet shirt off. He's not surprised when he feels Azure's hand running up the bare skin of his back and he already knows where this is going as he slips out of the rest of his wet clothing.

Azure's clothes join his a few seconds later, then he's pressed into the sandy shore as the warmth of Azure's body covers his own.

"You were with Dominicus yesterday." Azure's voice brings him back to the present and he shakes off the memory, silent when he realizes what Azure said. His heart stutters and it takes all his effort not to take a step back. He doesn't want to have this conversation yet, not before he's really had a chance to earn Azure's forgiveness. "Hope he enjoys being homeless and broke."

Ocher drops to his knees next to him, "Wait Azure. Don't do that."

"Why not? You're the one who broke your promise. Give me one reason I shouldn't."

"Because you love me?" Azure reaches out a hand to cradle the side of his face and he leans in eagerly, reaching up a hand to hold Azure's in place.

"Do I?"

"I want you to."

Azure looks at him, letting his thumb stroke against his cheek as he searches for something in the depths of his eyes. "I wanted to as well," he says quietly. "But you've never been trustworthy."

His stomach drops, does he know? "Azure…"

"Are you trustworthy?"

"What?"

"You heard me, are you or not?"

He could lie, but if he does and Azure finds out, and it's only a matter of time until he will, then it'll be double the strikes against him. Ocher looks away, "I'm not."

"I know." Azure withdraws his hand and turns back towards the lake. "Go away, you're bothering me."

Ocher stands and waits, hoping Azure will look back at him until he eventually gives up and walks away. He sighs, this is how it always is with them. They never come right out and say things, and he can't put all the blame on Azure because he's not willing to be honest either.

Eren and Erina find him once he steps back inside and the questions start up. Is he okay? What happened last night? *He* doesn't even know what happened last night. One moment he's fighting with Azure and the next, it's morning. Everything between that is blank.

What he does know is that he doesn't want to deal with them right now. He understands friends are supposed to worry about you and be on your side, the same way Basel and Sara are forever in sync with Azure, but this is still a new experience for him.

He finds it stressful, managing his own emotions and appeasing others. Now he understands why Azure rarely ever does it. Azure does what he wants and doesn't care about the effect on others, he's experienced that firsthand.

Dominicus approaches them shortly after he's reassured the twins that he's fine and if that's not the worst timing. Fingers brush against his and he represses the urge to flinch away and call attention to their hands. The twins may be more approving of Dominicus than they are to Azure, but he doesn't want to explain anything else to them. He can't even lie because Dominicus is right here too.

They're all so close to him and it's suffocating. He's not a nice person, so why do they all like him? Why does he have to bear their affections? He never struggled with Azure's affections, if anything, he wanted *more* from him.

Before he left, the *only* person he cared about emotionally was Azure. He wanted his attention and touches. Whenever he needed comfort, Azure never, not once, pushed him away.

He was allowed to crawl onto Azure and into his arms at any time no matter who was there and know he would always be welcomed. Grouchy, angry, happy, Azure never pulled away from him. What he wouldn't give for that now. He's starting to realize Azure indulged him an incredible amount. No wonder Sara always made fun of him.

Azure never seemed to mind if he was clingy or annoying or even somewhat whiny for attention, so how would he know he was being overindulged? He'd only ever turned to Azure for anything and now he doesn't know how to find comfort anywhere else.

Looking back, that might have been the sole intention of Azure giving him so much attention, to make sure he was so used to turning only to him that no one else ever crossed his mind to confide in. He never gave it a second thought at the time, Azure was just always there.

Savanta had tried to break him of that habit once, he remembers. She had tried to pull him away and talk to him when he was upset about something, but he wasn't interested in listening to her. Why would he be when he could stay there with Azure who would give him soft touches and affection until he felt better?

And probably some mental manipulation that he was ignorant of back then.

Everyday since he's been back, he understands a little more how much control he unwittingly let Azure have over him. It was always hidden under a facade of caring unless he pissed Azure off, then he was shunned and avoided.

Rarely could he take more than a day of that before he gave in to whatever Azure wanted from him, too desperate to be back in Azure's good graces where he felt loved. Part of him wishes he was still oblivious to Azure's careful manipulation of him because now he wonders, where does Azure draw the line between love and control?

It feels more and more like what he thought was love was actually a tool to control him once there was no longer the threat of being punished for defecting, and now that he's pulled away, Azure doesn't really want him anymore. Savanta did tell him once that the limits of Azure's tolerance of him depended on his lack of questioning.

He never should have come back here.

Dominicus' hand slides down his wrist to entwine their fingers loosely, and three pairs of worried brown eyes stare into his own. He can't take it anymore, he runs.

CHAPTER 11: AZURE

"We just want to know our brother."

"Too bad, maybe he doesn't want to know you," Azure says.

Ocher's brothers are here where they have no right to be, two years later with no invitation and no prior warning. They're not welcome here and if they wanted to see their 'brother' so badly, they've had two years to do it. He doesn't care what they want now. They're lucky Odaius never actually came for them.

No one gets to Ocher without going through him first and he's not letting them anywhere near him.

"That's not your choice," Eliam, Ocher's eldest brother, tells him.

"It's not yours either."

"Can we just speak to him?" Aren pleads.

"No." Azure holds firm. He doesn't owe them anything.

Eliam's gaze hardens. "You can't stop us."

"Are you that ignorant? I can. Leave and if you come back, I'll have you thrown in jail."

"We're his family, he wouldn't let you do that!"

Azure laughs harshly. "The fact that you think he wouldn't tells me that you don't know him at all. Ocher wouldn't say a thing about it. If I threw you in jail, he might not even bring it up."

"He's our *brother*."

Azure glares. Is that supposed to mean something to him? "I'm the only family he has or needs."

"But -"

"Escort them out!" He shouts to several of the guards lingering nearby. He's entertained them long enough.

They're trash. Why would Ocher want anything to do with them? He turned his back on them when he left them to die, but it looks like they dodged a bullet. He never cared enough to look up what happened to them and he doesn't know if Ocher did.

Seeing them is the last thing Ocher needs right now. He's already hiding something, he doesn't need more stress.

Azure breezes through the front yard and into the side garden, and as he passes by Eren and Erina's glares bore into him, no doubt still angry about their last meeting when they trespassed in his room. That's disrespect he won't take in his final days.

Normally, he would let it go, but being glared at in his own home when he allowed them to stay here free of charge?

Azure turns to them, "Spit out whatever it is you want to say."

"I wish he would stay away from you," Eren tells him without hesitation. "You're terrible to him and he doesn't deserve it. He deserves better than you."

"Oh yeah? And why is that, since you know him so well to know what he deserves?"

"Ocher is *nice.* He works hard and is kind to everyone. The only time he's ever been mean is when he's around *you.* You make him angry, then he gets mean. If you weren't around he'd be happier."

"Who do you think he is? Some innocent?" Azure questions in disbelief. Who the hell has Ocher been pretending to be for the past year? Azure laughs, "If you keep handling him like a child, you'll be in for a nasty surprise when he turns on you and punches you in the face."

"Ocher's not like that," Erina argues. "He's never hurt anyone!"

"Really?" Azure shakes his head. This is too ridiculous. "What do you even know about him? Where did he come from?"

"His family died when he was young and he was raised in a small fishing town. He wasn't a third son, so he never had to fight in the army. After Haithen's government changed, he decided to leave the village he was raised in and explore. He wandered around for a while." She gives him a dirty look. "I guess that's when he met you and then ended up settling in our town since he was already used to hard work."

Azure blinks. So Ocher essentially gave them his back story. If that's really the story he's telling, then Ocher has grown to be a liar just like him. "He didn't even tell me that."

Erina looks at him smugly, "Because he *trusts* us."

More like the opposite, but he won't unravel Ocher's lies just yet. He'll let them live with their delusions a little longer. "You say that, but he's still *here.*"

"The only reason he's staying here is because it's comfortable, not because of you."

"Of course he's comfortable here, it's his home!"

"What?"

"It's his home." Azure gestures to the entirety of the buildings and grounds. "Here in this place, with me. Whatever other bullshit he told you, that's a fact."

"He was fine staying away for a year, doesn't sound like home to me. Home is where you *want* to be."

"He wants to *be* here."

"No," Erina disagrees. "That's what you want and you can't make that choice for him. Ocher is free to live where he wants and love who he wants!"

"You would think that, wouldn't you? But he's really really not."

"You're arrogant if you think that he'd pick you."

Azure shakes his head, "You say that as if there's any choice. If I gave him an ultimatum, what do you think his answer would be? Do you really think he would pick you or brother over me?"

"We've been by his side for over a year helping him adjust to the world," Eren defends. "We've been there for him."

"And that's very nice of you, but that won't give you his heart and it doesn't mean he owes either of you anything."

"He doesn't owe you anything either."

"Then it's a good thing I'm not asking him for anything, but don't take it from me, go ask him. Let him answer you." They don't move and he notices the hesitation in the looks the two of them exchange. They don't believe what they're saying.

Azure walks away, he's tired. It's been another long day, like every day recently. Why is everyone so concerned about Ocher? No one used to care and now people are in his face, questioning him, sowing discord, and caring about Ocher's general well being. It's annoying and he looks forward to the day that he doesn't have to look at any of them ever again.

He can do what he pleases with Ocher. If they cared so much, they should have done something about it much earlier.

It's only evening, and he wishes there wasn't so much time before he could sleep. The energy thing is brutal. It gets worse everyday, especially after talking to people.

"There you are," Basel pushes open the door to his sitting room and joins him on the couch. Azure briefly considers kicking him out, but Basel is one of the least trying people. Basel glances around the room, "You're alone? Where's Ocher?"

"I don't know."

"You're not keeping tabs on him anymore? I'm surprised." Basel frowns in mock disappointment. "And you say he's your other half."

Azure sighs, "He's guilty."

"What do you mean?"

"He feels guilty about something he did, but he hasn't told me what."

"How do you know?"

"I can feel how stressed he is lately and he's already admitted that he's not trustworthy. Until he admits what he's done or what's upsetting him so much, I don't want him too close to me. I don't need the added worry."

Basel looks him over, "You do look tired."

"I really am."

"Still dying?"

"Yes."

Basel suddenly breaks into a grin, "Stressed out? When was the last time you…?"

Azure glares at him, "Like a year."

"Really? A whole year?" Basel laughs. "He's back and you still haven't been with him again. You two must be doing worse than I thought."

"It hasn't come up and I'm not going to force him into bed. Who knows what he's thinking?"

"Yeah," Basel smirks. "Bad."

"*No,* but Ocher is a crier."

"Is he?"

"Yeah," Azure shrugs. "You'd be surprised, seven out of ten times ends with him in tears."

Basel raises an eyebrow, hazel eyes sparkling mischievously, "I'm not."

Azure huffs out a laugh, "He'd kill us both."

"Try at least."

"And might succeed with you."

"Let's find out," Basel leans in towards him and Azure isn't *against* it. It would be easy with Basel, no strings attached and he's curious how far Basel will go if he doesn't stop him or if he's just joking around.

There's the faintest brush of lips against his, then Basel is pulling back with a slew of curse words. Azure opens his eyes and rolls off the couch right in time to avoid the fist aiming for him this time.

He backs up, raising his hands in the face of Ocher's red faced fury. "What's with you?"

"You!"

"I didn't even do anything!" He dodges Ocher's swinging fist and ducks out of the room, leaving Basel groaning on the floor at Ocher's mercy.

Some things never change.

CHAPTER 12: OCHER

Ocher storms through the mansion on a warpath searching for Azure. He's livid! He *hates* Basel and the fact that Azure would do that when he's here too? Azure hasn't kissed him again since Vita. So why *Basel?*

Azure is supposed to love *him.*

"Ocher, what's wrong?" He groans internally at the sound of Eren's voice, not them again. He's starting to think it was a mistake to let them stay here. "Hey, slow down," Eren charges after him and grabs him by the arm.

Unthinkingly, he shakes Eren's hand off and shoves him backwards. He doesn't want to be touched right now. Eren stumbles backwards into the fall from the force, clutching his chest. "Ow Ocher, what the hell?"

"...Sorry." Except he's really not. He didn't ask to be bothered right now.

Azure's laugh echoes from around the corner and he runs towards the sound, finally cornering the other boy in the hallway. "Azure."

"Yes?"

"Why?"

"Why what? I didn't even do anything." Azure didn't do anything because he showed up to interrupt him, and it makes him angrier that he can't say the same for himself. "We're not even together, what's it matter? You said yourself that you wanted independence."

Ocher glares, unable to argue with his statement. They're *not* together, but Azure will be just as mad as he is when he finds out about Dominicus. Azure is still *his* even when he's not and Basel can't have him.

Azure breaks their stare down to remove something from his pocket. He runs his fingers over the smooth obsidian of a bangle that he would recognize anywhere and Ocher's eyes widen. That's his! It's the only solid proof he had that Azure might actually love him. He treasured that gift from Azure more than anything.

He steps forward, "Give it back."

"Nope." Azure pulls it out of reach. "You gave it back when you left."

"No I didn't!"

"Then why is it here with me?" He asks calmly in the face of his rising anger.

"I couldn't find it...did you *take* it?"

"Maybe, who cares, you left. You didn't need it. You were perfectly happy to leave everything behind and start a new life. Basel always asked me to get him one, so I guess it doesn't matter."

There's no way *in hell* that he'll let Azure give his gift to Basel. "Give it back."

"Why should I? Maybe you should get one from Erina. I'm sure she'd love it if you wore something she gave you."

"Azure, that's mine."

"Not anymore, it isn't. You don't deserve it. You left without it, now it belongs to me and whoever I want to give it to."

"No, it doesn't!" He charges forward and Azure keeps him back with a firm hand to the chest.

"Do you really think someone like *you* is worthy of this? You can't even be bothered to stick around. Maybe you should just go back wherever you came from and stay there. I don't think I want you here anymore."

It hurts to hear Azure say that to him, to tell him so straightforwardly that he's not welcome. Azure is the only person he's ever wanted and he's constantly refused now. He hates this. He feels the beginning of a faint stinging in his eyes, and he needs to get out of here. Azure can't see him that upset.

"I'll leave, just give it back first." He reaches for the bangle and Azure holds it further out of reach.

"No, leave without it. And when you leave, take your little harem with you. Eren, Erina, Dominicus, take all of them. I'm sure they'd all enjoy *being* with you. And who knows maybe you'd actually enjoy it, since you seem to like pleasing everyone so much now. I'm sure they'd like that. You always were easy."

He blinks, stunned at Azure's words. He feels stung at the cruelty of his words, at the implications. The burn of frustrated tears pricks at his eyes, but letting Azure see him cry would make this so much worse.

Basel plucks the bangle from Azure's hand and holds it out to him. "Go easy on him, Azure." Ocher takes it from him, letting the bangle hang limply from his fingers.

Azure won't even look at him.

"Why should I?" He leans in and peers at Basel's face. "He did *that* to your eye."

"I'll heal."

Azure smiles, "Want some help?"

"Which help are you offering?"

They ignore him now, flirting as if he's not even there. He might as well not be, nothing would change. He can't take watching them any longer and he doesn't want to walk past them, so he escapes out the side door onto an empty balcony.

Outside, he lets one quiet sob escape him. He's not sure how much longer he can take being near Azure without his forgiveness, especially when everything Azure says seems designed to hurt him. His head is aching. He regrets kissing Dominicus more than anything right now. It makes him a hypocrite with no claim to Azure.

He looks down at the bangle he finally has again after a year and slides it onto his wrist. What is he supposed to do? What decision can he make? He's going to be thrown away permanently. And his choices? Eren, Erina, or Dominicus, he wouldn't pick any of them, but then he'd really be alone.

Ocher takes a breath. The longer he stays out here, the harder it'll be to go back, maybe everyone will have cleared out. Ocher pulls the doors open and steps into the hallway, looking both ways to confirm it's empty. He wants to get to his room without running into anyone.

The hallways are quiet as he makes his way through the mansion. A few workers pass by and none give him a second look. He climbs up the stairs, turns left, and freezes abruptly. They're all here.

Erina reaches out a hand to him and he steps out of reach. He doesn't want her touch either. She can't comfort him.

Sara sees him and her smile changes to sympathy at the sight of his red rimmed eyes. She looks between him and Azure, "What did you do, Azure?"

"Who said I did anything?" Azure still won't look at him. "I've just been here talking to Basel."

"Basel?"

"He was an ass, what else is new?" Basel answers, honest for once.

Sara grabs hold of his wrist, ignoring his flinch, and pulls him down the hall. "Let's go talk, Ocher."

"Sara," Azure calls out as she leads him towards her room. "I thought you should know Savanta told me why you're here."

"Don't be such an ass, Azure!" She calls back.

"Just reminding you."

They end up in Sara's bed, laying shoulder to shoulder. "Go ahead, tell me what happened. You only get this upset when he does something."

Ocher turns to look at her, "It's hard, Sara. He's *everything.* There's no halves with him, it's all or nothing. I can't...I just...and...I kissed Dominicus. We're done forever, if he finds out."

Sara sucks in a breath, "Then why did you do it?"

"I don't know. He's my friend, and he was my only one for so long. He wanted to and Azure was mad at me, so I just did."

She sighs, "Azure really didn't let you grow much at all when you were with him, did he?"

"I don't know. Part of me kind of liked it when he took care of everything."

"And how's that working out for you now?"

He looks at her, "I'm going crazy. I think...he probably messed with my head to keep me calm."

"Hmm, how so?"

She doesn't know? Then he's not going to say anything either. "Just a thought."

"He *is* going to be angry when he finds out." Even Sara knows he always finds out one way or another when it comes to him.

"Tell me something about Azure," he begs desperately. "Something he doesn't want people to know, something he hates."

Sara laughs, "I can't give you his weaknesses and if I did, he would find something extremely unpleasant to do to me. Savanta wouldn't even be able to stop him."

"But, I'm..."

"You're what? You insist you're not dating. You two can't be called friends, so what exactly are you to him? It's important when you're going around kissing other guys."

She's right. Right now, they're nothing. He had hoped going to Vita with Azure would help them move towards forgiveness, but it feels like everyday Azure gets farther away from him. "It's not fair that he knows everything about me."

"What do you expect? He knows all your triggers, what you do or don't like, where you like to be touched. You let him take you apart and you didn't hold anything back."

He ignores the fact that she knows about those times, he's not surprised. Azure *talks* to his friends. He can only hope she doesn't know the full details of how he lay bare in front of Azure, letting his mouth and hands draw every thought and emotion from him until all parts of him were exposed. "He didn't *let* me hold things back."

"I know, and you never asked him to give you as much vulnerability as you gave him. It's not your fault though, he's been taking advantage of you from the very beginning."

"I hate this."

"You still want him," Sara states, hearing the words he doesn't want to say. She pats his head in understanding at his silence. "It'll get better," she tells him and he allows himself to fall asleep under her gentle hand.

He stirs awake in the dead of night to an empty bed. Sara's side is cold. He rises and his feet are taking him down a familiar path before his mind catches up. The nondescript dark wood door is the same as the others in this hall, but everything he wants is behind it.

Before he can tell himself this is a bad idea, he steels himself and creeps into Azure's dark bedroom. He crouches next to Azure's bed, gently shaking him until dark eyes crack open and rest on him in silence.

"Stop, *please* Azure."

"Stop what? You'll have to be clearer than that."

"Azure, *please*," he begs. "I'm yours, I promise."

Azure sits up, abruptly shoving him away from the bed. "You made that same promise before and then you left. Why should I ever believe you again?"

He pushes down the hurt at being shoved away. "Because I -"

"You cater to every person here and you're split. You're not mine, you're just saying that to get what you want. Basel was right, you just can't function without my attention. Don't act like I can't see right through you. *You're not mine.*"

Ocher feels each of his last words stabbing into his heart through their bond. There's true anger there, Azure means what he's saying and it feels like he's drowning. Wetness drips down his cheeks, and he can barely get a breath through his sobs.

He would throw all of them away if it meant they could go back to how they were before. If Azure would just *listen* to him and let him fix this, they could be good again.

Azure flinches and he feels the parallel pain in his chest. Maybe if Azure could feel what he feels, he would know that he's sincere. He needs to let him know, he needs for them to be together again.

Ocher reaches out a hand at the same time he reaches for their bond, pushing his feelings through it.

Azure knocks his hand away, "Don't you dare. I don't want to feel what you feel." Ocher pushes harder, desperate to break through the mental shield Azure has enforced between them. Azure jumps out of bed and pins him to the floor, "I told you *no*."

A hand presses roughly against his face, then everything goes black.

CHAPTER 13: AZURE

They came back.

As if his cosmic karma wasn't already doing enough in his last days to make him atone.This is probably punishment for how he treated Ocher, but in his defense, he was woken up in the middle of the night when he was already tired *and* nothing he said was wrong.

Ocher tries to avoid conflict by either hiding from people or lying. He's lied to the twins so much that all he has to do is breathe and the facade he puts up begins to crack.

He should stop. It's unbelievable that he hasn't realized by now that Azure's opinion is the one that should matter the most to him, everyone else should be an afterthought at best.

Azure stares at Ocher's two brothers, once again in his front yard. They didn't bring the sister this time either, that makes this easier. "You actually returned even after I told you what would happen. I see the same stupidity Ocher possesses runs in the family."

"Don't talk about him that way," Eliam says. "If you think so little of him, you should let us visit him."

"Did you think you would get to see him?" Azure asks curiously. He can't fathom what about his personality or his actions would make them think he would give in.

"We were actually hoping you wouldn't be here this time."

Azure smiles, "Doesn't matter. If I wasn't here, you still wouldn't be allowed in. I told you, all requests go through me." He waves a guard over, "Lock them up."

"You were serious?"

"I was fully behind him leaving you to die to save himself, what made you think I was joking? If you wanted to talk to him, then you should have done it before he came back to me."

Basel approaches him as their shouts ring through the yard. The guards don't care, continuing to drag them towards the basement levels. "That's not the way to the entrance."

"They're not leaving. I gave them a chance, now they're being locked up."

He blinks between Azure and the shouting brothers, "What crime did they commit?"

"The crime of making me look at them."

Basel gives a short laugh. "That's cold, even for you. Who are they?"

"Ocher's brothers."

"Azure, what?" He does a second take. "You're locking up his family?

"I told them that if they came back, I would throw them in jail and they did, so now I'm keeping my word. You said I lie too much anyway."

"That's not what I meant and you know it. What did they want?"

"To see him."

"And…?"

"And I said no."

"Azure, you can't keep his family from him."

"I just did."

"Does he know?"

"No, besides they're not even his family. Ocher doesn't want anything to do with them."

"Shouldn't he get a choice?"

Azure looks at him, "I think Ocher has had enough choices in the past year and he's proven that he makes bad decisions."

"And if they want to make amends?"

"They can make amends over my dead body."

"Highly likely that's what will happen." Azure makes a face and reaches up to Basel's swollen eye, healing it with a quick burst of energy. "Oh wow, that's much better. It's only right that you fix it since it's your fault he did it."

"I didn't tell you to try and kiss me."

"You didn't tell me no either."

Azure shrugs. "I don't make decisions for you."

"Yeah, yeah. Should you really be using like that?"

"I might as well do something decent in my last days."

Basel shakes his head, "Come on leader, war meeting."

They step into the meeting room and all eyes turn to them. "Glad to see you're finally joining us again," Kronos greets.

"That makes one of us."

"Do you even try?" Basel questions, nudging him aside to take a seat. "He didn't mean that."

"We're all quite sure he did," Kronos replies. "However his personal feelings don't really matter as much as fulfilling his responsibilities. I assume Basel has filled you in on our decision?"

"He has."

"From Basel's report we know that the threat is the royal family, not the citizens. However, even inexperienced citizens can overpower us if there's enough of them. The citizen's are extremely loyal through brainwashing and will fight to the death to defend them."

Azure gives Basel a confused look and he shrugs helplessly. Apparently he decided brainwashing would be easier for them to take than the truth. He supposes he can understand that because if they knew, then they might wonder if he possessed that same ability and that would make their dislike of him stronger.

"Azure, can you handle enough of the citizens for us to target the royal family?"

Can he handle them all? *No.* Three of them and with them possibly controlling who knows how many citizens each, he'd have to just kill them all and he really doesn't want to do that.

He turns to Dominicus, "Get out."

Dominicus looks at him in surprise, "I need to be here for the details?"

"Someone will fill you in."

"I understand personal issues with me, but this involves our country's safety," he protests.

"Get. Out," he bites out. Yes, he does have personal issues with Dominicus, but now isn't the time to discuss them. And in reality, Dominicus shouldn't want to discuss anything with him either because it would probably end with him losing his job which he's only keeping by a hairsbreadth now.

No one else speaks up or comes to his defense, so with a last look around the room, he steps out with a frown and shuts the door behind him.

Azure addresses the room. "I appreciate Basel giving the short version, but in truth, they possess similar abilities to me. Someone in Meio told me a group split off and went east earlier, I believe they settled in Vita. I don't know if they founded Vita or took over, but they're in charge now."

Chaos breaks out in the room with angry shouts being thrown in Basel's direction for lying to them and potentially leading them into a slaughter from lack of understanding. He gets their annoyance, but they're the ones who want to fight. Neither he nor Basel owe them the truth about anything if they choose otherwise.

"Shut up. I'm not done talking," Azure interrupts, cutting across the noise. "I have the suspicion that the royal family exerts mental control over everyone when they need to. There's at least twenty of them, including the ones enforcing other areas of the country. Maybe a few illegitimates with latent powers, they shouldn't matter. Either way, I can't stand against that many. If you go against them, you'll need enough soldiers to stand against several of me, provided you end it before the rest of the family can be called to the capital, and their own soldiers or citizens as well."

Basel looks at him as if he's suddenly grown a third head, "It's that serious? You acted like it was no big deal!"

"It's not, to me. If Haithen goes underprepared, we'll lose and Vita will probably take over. I'm just giving them the facts, I don't care what they decide."

"Then we'll mobilize the entire army," Kronos decides and the others murmur assent. "We won't wait for them to come to us. Every soldier not stationed here will be reassigned to prepare for Vita's advances."

"Fine, but I'm not going. Decide the strategy yourselves. He pushes his chair back and leaves, letting the door shut on their protests. They should understand by now that he doesn't care.

Dominicus stands outside the door and Azure spitefully hopes that he gets sent to the frontlines.

CHAPTER 14: OCHER

He woke up on the couch to Azure glaring down at him. "Don't try that again," he said. "I don't like that."

"So? You never cared what I liked?" He challenged.

Azure scoffed at him. "I never cared what you liked? Then it's funny how much I managed to indulge you without knowing exactly what you like. Don't lie to make yourself feel better. Of course I cared. Not now, though."

"I shouldn't have left."

"No, you shouldn't have, but you did. For a year. So you don't get to complain anymore, understand?"

"Yeah."

And now he's here, curled up in the grass of the back gardens, half hidden in the narrow space between a hedge and flowers. It's his favorite spot to think, and he hasn't been back here in over a year. The small space is shaded with just enough room for him and no one ever finds him back here.

Well, almost no one. Azure always finds him, no matter where he is, so he doesn't count.

Then, depending on how Azure felt at the time, he would either drag him out or squeeze in on top of him until both of them were crowded into the too narrow space. He misses that type of companionship, when Azure was softer with him.

"Ocher, come in." Azure tells him, swimming lazily through the lake. He refuses, content where he is on the edge with only his feet in the water.

"It's too deep," he calls back.

"Which is why you should come in now when I'm here. You'll have to learn to swim eventually."

"No, I won't. There is no reason for me to learn how."

"What if I'm swimming through the ocean, farther and farther away, and you're stuck on shore alone? Then what?"

"You would come back," Ocher says with complete confidence. "You wouldn't leave me there."

Azure laughs, "You're not wrong, but I'd still prefer if you were with me." He swims over, moving through the water easily. Azure comes up for air in front of him, long hair plastered to his face, and reaches forward to pull him into a tight hug.

Without thinking, Ocher hugs him back. He only realizes it for the trap it is when Azure lifts him and kicks backward, dragging him into the cold lake. "Azure!"

"What? I feel like you should've seen that coming."

"No!" His legs kick desperately to keep him afloat and his arms stay locked around Azure. Like most of the time since they met, he's completely at the grace of Azure's mercy. "Take me back?"

"But I like the water and I like you, I should be able to enjoy both together for a little while."

Ugh. Azure always knows what to say to get what he wants. "Just for a little. It's still cold."

Azure graces him with a wide smile and brushes back his wet hair to kiss him on the forehead with fond eyes. "You should always stay with me."

"Where else am I going to go?" He mutters.

He hums in agreement and abruptly lets go, letting him sink into cold darkness. Ocher flails, sucking in a lungful of water before he's blessed with air again. He can hear Azure laughing over his attempts to cough the water from his lungs.

Cool hands cradle his face and a mouth covers his, followed by the odd tickling sensation of the last drops of water being pulled from his body. "Better?"

"No!" He goes to glare and realizes he can barely see Azure. They're still in the lake, encapsulated in water, and resting on the lake bed. The light of the sun is far above them. He shifts in the sand, "You better not lose control."

"Like I would ever let you drown." The words are spoken against his neck as Azure moves closer in the murky darkness.

"What are we doing down here? Is this why you insisted I come out here with you?"

"Have you ever had sex at the bottom of a lake?"

"Seriously!" Ocher pushes him away and stands, feeling his toes dig into the damp sand. Azure obviously knows the answer to that, all his sexual experience is with him. "Is that all you ever think about?"

"Of course I don't only think about sex, it's mostly sex with you."

Ocher makes a noise of frustration. Over the past few months, it's become increasingly clear that Azure loves sex, and sometimes he almost almost wishes that Azure would take it out on someone else because they're complete opposites in that regard.

"Please?" Azure tugs at his shorts. "How many people can say they've had this experience?"

He rolls his eyes, "How long am I going to be stuck down here until I agree?"

"Not that...long."

Ocher drops to his knees, reaching out blindly until Azure pulls him into his lap. "You're such an ass."

He doesn't respond, already busy slipping his hand below his waistband.

Ocher almost laughs at that memory, it actually hadn't been a bad experience and they'd stayed down there in that small intimate space made just for them for much longer than he'd expected. By the time Azure brought them back up, it was almost dusk.

How did he let things move from that easy to so complicated? Why couldn't he figure things out by staying here? Now somehow he's dealing with the emotions of four different people, it's exhausting.

He's learning the hard way that maintaining a good impression and trying to, or at least pretending to care about everyone is hard. He doesn't want to hurt anyone, but he can't keep up with their expectations here. There are too many people here that know him.

And of course, the one person who refuses to let him have any peace.

All Azure ever demanded from him was unconditional devotion and it wasn't hard to give until he decided he wanted to make his own choices.

Someone else had controlled his life for almost the entire time he's been alive. He went from the army, and then straight to Azure. It's not his fault that he wanted to try something else, but making your own choices isn't as great as he'd thought.

The transition was hard, Azure had been close for so long that leaving and finding somewhere to belong seemed like a monumental task. But, once he overcame that, living near the farm was fine. He was still always a little lonely though, unwilling to form more than a platonic relationship with anyone else. There was too much he didn't want people to know.

He misses being loved, even if that wasn't what it really was. He misses having someone who knew every part of him and still loved him with no facades between them. Maybe that's it. The other three don't know him as well, they don't know what he's capable of, so how can he really trust them?

He's never opened himself up to them and there's no guarantee that they'll like what they find. Dominicus hasn't even fully realized the type of person he's turned into.

For all that Azure treats him like a burden, he's still here and he's not really sure why. Azure resists most attempts to get close to him again, but sometimes he gives in. He *knows* Azure doesn't hate him, despite his actions, because of those times.

That's why Azure still lets him sleep in his bed sometimes, why he hasn't been thrown out, and why he's still allowed to be near him if he doesn't push too far. He just has to find out what's holding Azure back and if anyone knows, it's Basel.

"Ocher?" A feminine voice calls. "Are you here?"

He recognizes Savanta's voice, similar to Sara's, but older and firmer. He waits until her footsteps move past his spot before slipping out and following behind her.

She stops at his approach, "There you are."

"How did you know I was here?"

"I didn't, but Azure mentioned before that you spend time back here."

"Oh." Of course he did, too bad Azure doesn't actually talk to him half as much. "What do you need?"

She looks at him for a moment as if deciding if she wants to speak. He wishes she'd hurry up. Savanta's gaze always made him nervous, like she was seeing every terrible part of him and either judging or pitying him. "Ocher, your brothers are in jail."

"What?" They can't be. They're not dead? What did they do? Have they been locked up for an entire two years? "Where?"

"Here."

"*Here?* For how long?"

"They haven't been here long." She exhales. "Azure didn't tell you." She says that as if she shouldn't be surprised. "He had them thrown in jail for wanting to talk to you."

That sounds exactly like Azure. "So...those people aren't dead?"

"No. I think your whole family is alive."

"They're not my family," he corrects immediately.

"Okay. Do you want them released?"

Does he want them released so they can come talk to him? No. Dealing with more people is the last thing he wants, definitely not them. He doesn't want to hear anything they have to say. He left them to their fate and never intended to see them again. "Not really."

"You're okay with leaving them there?"

"I don't want to see them. Who else knows?"

"Sara was there when we heard the guards talking about it, but she wouldn't tell you. She's too loyal to Azure. They stopped talking when they saw us nearby."

"Where's Azure?"

"I'm not sure. Will you free them?"

Will he go against Azure's orders for people he doesn't even want to know? No. They're not worth it to him. "I'll...talk to him."

"Ocher, are you okay?"

"Yes...no. I wish you hadn't told me. I don't want to be responsible for them. I'm always upset now."

"That's because you're under a lot of stress and Azure won't help you. You were already a little emotionally unstable before you two broke up."

"What? How do you know that?" Why does she know things he doesn't?

"Azure talks about you a lot. Did you really think he wouldn't ever mention you? Ocher, he might not admit it, but he doesn't only have his nails in you, it's vice versa."

"Then why didn't he stop me from leaving?" He asks before he can catch himself. "If he cared so much, why did he practically force me out the door?"

"Why would he stop you when you made it clear that you wanted to leave? Azure will never fight for someone who doesn't want him, ever."

"I wish he'd talk to me, just *once* like he talks to you and Basel."

"I know. He's difficult. It's still not too late to leave, you know."

"You've been trying to get me to leave him since the beginning."

She nods. "You didn't listen and look where you are now."

"I'm going to find Azure."

"Okay."

◆ ◆ ◆

He finds Azure on the second floor talking with Basel, the only other person he wants to see right now. They're speaking about military strategy, but he doesn't care for the details. He was glad to leave that part of his life behind and he's never looked back.

"Azure," Ocher wraps arounds him and rests against his side.

"Yeah, what is it?"

He doesn't respond and Azure doesn't ask again, simply hugs him back and returns to speaking with Basel without a second thought. Fingers press along his torso and he buries his face in Azure's neck. It seems like no matter how bad of terms they're on, Azure still won't deny him comfort.

Basel gags behind him and he presses in tighter. Screw Basel.

"I don't know why you keep him around," Basel says and Ocher can tell he means it to be antagonizing to him.

"What's not to like? He's cute, loyal, and he's got a soft mouth. Don't you, Ocher?" Azure teases before grabbing his face and kissing him soundly.

All of his words are for Basel's benefit, he knows Azure doesn't think that positively of him. Ocher kisses him back hard anyway because Azure wouldn't do it if he knew how disloyal he'd been.

"Spare me. Can you pry him off so we can finish talking?"

Ocher steps back, not because he thinks Azure will pry him off, but because he wants them to finish as soon as possible so he can try to get answers from Basel. He heads to Basel's room to wait, it would be too suspicious if he hung around there waiting for him.

He doesn't have to wait too long before Basel pushes open the door, pausing when he catches sight of Ocher sitting in a chair. "Did you get confused?"

"No, I was waiting for you."

Basel stares at him. He understands. The two of them aren't usually alone together. "Don't think you can use me as a replacement for Azure," he finally says. "I can't stand the thought of how much coddling he does with you."

He grimaces, "I wouldn't want you to."

"I mean, don't get me wrong. I don't like you, but I'd still sleep with you if that's what you wanted." Ocher gags, the thought alone is enough to make him cringe. There's almost nothing he wants less. "Then, hurry up and tell me what you want before I call the guards to throw you out."

Ocher looks at him skeptically, "You really think they'd throw me out?" He doesn't think they would.

"Ugh, you're right. They probably wouldn't. You're Azure's, they wouldn't lay a finger on you."

Speaking of Azure, he gets to the point. "Why won't he forgive me?"

"What? Have you met the guy? He can hold a grudge for a lifetime."

"I know that, but he doesn't hate me or I wouldn't be here right now," Ocher points out. "So, why won't he accept me back? What's stopping him?"

"Well, well, well," Basel smirks at him and sits cross legged on his bed. "Everything not so perfect anymore?"

"You know it's not."

"And instead of asking Azure, you came to me, his best friend."

He doesn't need the reminder. "Will you just tell me?"

Basel's smirk suddenly drops and he studies him almost sympathetically, "Are you sure you want to know?"

"Yes." And he braces for the answer.

"Maybe because you've been gone a year and I slept with him. Why would he let you back in when I'm right here and better? And I don't cry either." Ocher's stomach drops, it's the one thing he didn't want. "We were together before you came along, you know? *You're* the extra person."

He thinks he's going to be sick and hopefully all over Basel's room. He hates Basel for this, but truthfully he knows he can't blame either one of them. It's his fault. He's the one that left.

"Don't look so sad. At least he still lets you live here even though you dragged two other people along with you."

"Shut up. I don't need comfort from you."

"Oh, I'm not comforting you," Basel corrects. "I'm reminding you that you're lucky he lets you stay here. Besides, comfort wise, all I could say is that at least I waited a few weeks after you left before I approached him again."

"Again?"

"You don't seriously think we stopped just because you were around, do you?"

He goes cold. That can't be true. "How...?" When? He was *always* with Azure or at least he thought he was. He tends to sleep earlier than Azure, could it have been then? If it's true, then Azure *didn't* care about him, certainly didn't love him.

"I'm kidding," Basel laughs. "Azure hates cheaters. "I definitely waited until you were gone!"

"That's not funny!" None of this is! His emotions are being played with for Basel's amusement and he hates that Basel knows exactly what to say to piss him off.

"What's funny is you thinking he'll ever come back to you. He won't, no matter how many times you give him those sad eyes!"

Ocher launches himself at Basel, going for his throat, anything to stop him from talking. Basel wedges a pillow between them, laughing. "You're not a substitute for Azure either. We were together right here on this bed, although our positions were reversed!"

He screams in frustration, pounding at Basel in a flurry of fists when he can't reach his throat through the pillow. He wants him to hurt just as badly as he does right now. His fist finally makes contact and he punches harder, ignoring the wet spots starting to pepper the pillow's surface, and in the next moment, someone grabs hold of him, pinning his arms to his sides and dragging him off Basel. He tries to break free and wipe that shit eating grin off Basel's face, but the arms around him tighten and pull him farther away.

"What are you doing in here, Ocher?" He stills, recognizing

Azure's voice and he's not sure he can face him now without breaking down. "Ocher?"

"Oh, now he's quiet," Basel snarks. "A minute ago, he couldn't stop talking."

Azure's fingertips trace under his eyes, wiping away the lingering wetness, "What were you two talking about?"

Basel raises an eyebrow. "Worried? Don't want me telling your secrets to your other half?"

"You wouldn't because I know yours as well."

Ocher tenses. What did Basel just call him? Azure's other half, and Azure didn't even deny it. Is that how he used to be thought of? Azure was really that fond of him? What has he done? He ruined everything.

Basel's grin grows wider, "Ocher just wanted to know why you refuse to love him again."

Azure's arms stiffen around him, "And what did you say?"

"I told him the truth, of course. You're the liar, deceiving him, not me."

Azure is silent and when he finally drags his eyes up to meet his deep blue gaze, Azure looks at him with something almost akin to guilt and that's all the confirmation of Basel's words that he needs.

He pulls away, feeling all his hopes disappear. It's over.

"Ocher!" Azure calls his name as he takes off out of Basel's room, but for the first time, he ignores Azure. There's nothing left to say.

CHAPTER 15: AZURE

"Savanta told Ocher about his brothers," Sara says in greeting as she flops down beside him on the library couch. He never gets peace when he has so many guests.

"That was a mistake on her part."

"Because you didn't want him to know?"

"No, because I can tell he's barely hanging on."

Her eyes brighten with curiosity. "Really?"

"Yeah...I think he's struggling with some things, maybe with his friends. I don't know, he hasn't told me what. I also think being attacked in Vita really messed with his head. Usually, I would help him deal with whatever's wrong, but he resisted me when I tried and I don't have the energy to fight him on it."

"Is that why he attacked Basel in his room?"

"I don't know that either. He's avoiding me and Basel still won't say exactly what he told Ocher." Azure exhales in frustration. He's not used to being this helpless and unaware of what's going on. He's used to being in control and now, no one is telling him anything.

"Poor Azure, not in charge of anything anymore. The council makes decisions without you, your best friend won't tell you things, and the boy you love is hiding from you. Sad times."

He shoots her an annoyed look, "What do you want, Sara?"

"It's time for lunch."

"Then *please* leave."

"You're coming too. You haven't been eating much or showing your face. As the host, you should eat with us."

Of course he hasn't made it a point to see everyone. He doesn't want to waste his limited time left interacting with people. "Who is *us*?"

"Everyone."

Too much. "Do I have to?"

"Come *on!* We barely see you anymore and we came all the way here to visit!"

"I guess the fact that you want to travel had nothing to do with your visit."

"I can have multiple reasons for wanting to see you!"

"If I go, will you leave me alone for the rest of the day?" He pauses. "And make sure everyone else does too?"

She rolls her eyes. "Fine, but you have to play nice the whole time too." Sara grabs his hand to pull him up and drags him towards the door. "What's wrong with you anyway? You've been grouchier than usual."

"That's just his personality. As he gets older, he gets more ornery with age," another voice comments.

"Ha, imagine when he's forty."

"If he lives that long," Basel replies with a meaningful look in his direction.

"Very true," Sara nods. "Azure has a way of making people angry."

"Must be why he looks so exhausted right now. Shouldn't you be resting?"

"I can handle lunch," Azure answers.

Sara looks at him in concern, "Are you sick?"

"Recovering."

"Mhmm." She looks him over, no doubt thinking about his propensity for lying before deciding to leave it alone and continue down the hall. "Are you coming to eat too, Basel?"

"Of course, Azure was hiding away, so I picked all the food. There's *nothing* raspberry flavored."

"What's that mean?"

"It's Ocher's favorite food."

"Ah." She laughs. "You two will do anything to make his life harder, give him a break sometimes. Azure says he's close to falling apart."

Basel lights up, "Is he?"

"*Basel,*" Azure warns. He's in full agreement with Sara, Basel's already harassed Ocher enough for the week, worse because he hasn't been allowed to hug him afterwards.

Sara pulls him to the dining room and he catches the tail end of Basel's smirk that tells him this is going to go badly. He doesn't want to be here.

He steps through the door and immediately his eyes lock on Ocher's, which is why he can see the exact moment fury overtakes him when Basel leans over to kiss him on the cheek. Sara's hand tightens around him in the tense atmosphere, then Ocher's shoving his chair back and focusing on Basel with a look that says he's ready to cause pain.

Azure pulls away from both of them, switching into a placating mode that he instinctively knows is useless right now without knowing why Ocher's so easily irritated. He'd assumed Ocher would use that year to grow, but looking at him right now, it's obvious he still hasn't learned to deal with any strong emotions.

He can see the anger building in the other boy's eyes and in his clenched fists. Azure had seen this coming from a mile away. The agitation, the begging, the constant annoyance, his head is probably spinning with too many emotions to sort through on his own. He'd rarely ever had to.

This meltdown was days in coming, building up until he can't pretend he's okay anymore. Erina reaches out a gentle hand to his shoulder to calm him and he shakes her off briskly. "Don't touch me," he snaps. Ocher stares straight at him, "I hate you."

"More like hates your attention being on anyone else," Basel mutters behind him and Azure shoots him a brief glare.

"No, you don't," Azure says. "But if you do...I'll leave with them and give you your space. I won't even complain if you leave with your friends and don't come back. I won't bother you again."

It's the wrong thing to say to make him feel better, but the right thing for the reaction he wants. Ocher charges at him and he steps forward to catch him easily, restraining him and ignoring his struggles until they're out of the room and far enough away from everyone else.

Azure releases him and pushes him away. "Tell me what's wrong," he demands. "No more lying. Tell me now." He's tired of this.

Ocher's anger drains away and he looks at him with scared eyes. "It's nothing."

"Ocher, tell me the truth or I'll drag it out of you." He's not sure if he can do that, but he's going to try.

He takes a step back, shrinking in on himself and says in a quiet voice, "I kissed Dominicus."

Azure stills. This little asshole. He's *guilty.* That's what his problem is. He was desperately begging for forgiveness while drowning in guilt and the fear that he would be found out. No wonder he's been so off the past few days.

Ocher clutches at his arm, "You can't be mad, you slept with Basel!"

"No, I didn't." Azure shakes him off. "Is that what he told you?" Ocher's silence and the dimming in his eyes is answer enough. "I don't know why you would believe him, he doesn't even like you."

Azure feels himself growing colder, he doesn't need this shit. If he's going to die anyway and Ocher has made his decision for him, then he supposes this is where they end.

"Don't worry about it. It doesn't matter." Azure steps away. "If you want to be with him, you can."

"I don't! Azure, I'm sorry! It was just once!"

"I won't even have him fired," Azure continues over him. "And you don't have to stay here any longer. Good luck with your life." He turns away to the sound of Ocher crying, refusing to turn back around. If he looks into those tear filled eyes, he might actually give in.

Ocher definitely knew this would happen, no wonder he admitted that he wasn't trustworthy. Well, all of this is over now. He pulls an employee aside and sends them off with a message to Basel.

He's through here.

There's a small packed bag sitting in his chair, ready for him to grab in the morning and the window is open, letting a slight breeze blow through the room when Ocher creeps silently through his door.

Maybe he can't sleep either. It would serve him right.

The moon illuminates his silhouette as he moves through the

dark and climbs into bed next to him. He's bold for someone whose secret just came out a few hours ago. Ocher squeezes in close to him, pressing their lips together until Azure finally acknowledges his presence.

Azure doesn't shove him away, waiting to see what Ocher wants. He can be nice since this is it, let Ocher know how badly he screwed up once he's dead.

"I'm sorry, Azure," he whispers.

"What for? We're not together, that's what you said, right? You're free to do what you want." Ocher's so close that he can feel the tremor that runs through his body at his words. "Did you sleep with him too?"

"No, I didn't! I swear!"

"Fine, I'll believe you," Azure huffs. "Even though your word doesn't mean much." He pushes Ocher onto his back and climbs on top of him.

He doesn't resist as Azure begins to undress him and Ocher knows he's not forgiven, but he'll let him do this anyway because he's weak that way. By the time Azure pushes in, the telltale signs of tears are already gathering in the corners of his eyes.

"Are you crying again?" Azure sighs, "You never change. I could understand if you were crying because it hurts, but you're not."

"I'm sorry," he sobs.

"Stop saying that." Azure shakes his head and gathers Ocher into his arms to cradle him close. "It's fine, cry if you need to," he says as he feels the cool wetness of tears sliding against his bare skin.

He shifts and Ocher jerks in his arms, gasping softly. And Ocher definitely hasn't done this in a while. At least he was honest about one thing. Azure presses him back down into the bed and begins to move in earnest, drawing soft noises from Ocher as they move together.

Ocher shudders underneath him and he follows soon after, collapsing onto the bed and allowing Ocher to curl against him and press his wet face into his neck. Azure runs a hand soothingly over Ocher's heated skin, this may very well be the last time they do this.

"Azure, I really am sorry." He feels Ocher's words said against his skin, but he doesn't reply. He's tired of hearing those words and at this point, they don't matter anymore.

What's done is done.

He rises early before dawn has even begun to lighten the sky. Azure dresses, grabs his bag, and heads for the door. One final look around his room is all he takes. Ocher still remains in his bed, asleep with deep, even breaths, unaware that he's leaving. His face is slack in sleep, tear streaked and exhausted with the beginnings of marks in several spots along his neck and chest.

As it should be, as it should have always stayed.

Azure shuts the door and Basel is waiting for him just on the other side. "You ready?" The other boy questions. "It'll be just like old times."

"And you're still an asshole."

Basel laughs, "I learned from the best."

CHAPTER 16: OCHER

Azure is gone, left him in his bed and disappeared with Basel in the early hours of the morning. He woke up alone and he's so cold inside. Receiving Azure's forgiveness was a distant dream, but he never thought Azure would be the one to leave his home instead of him. Last night wasn't enough to make him stay.

Remaining here now is too much. He can't be here in this place without Azure.

He doesn't know where Azure has gone, but he doubts Azure plans to come back especially after he confessed his guilt. Everything truly has fallen apart now.

The council doesn't know if they're coming back either and they yell at him for both not knowing and not stopping him. As if Azure is his responsibility, as if he has any control over what Azure chooses to do.

Haithen is angry that both Azure and Basel left them high and dry. No notes, no plans, no help, nothing. Azure doesn't typically care about how the country is run, but this is another level even for him.

"You really don't know where he went?" Eren asks. "They're angry."

Ocher thinks he's more aware of that than Eren is. "No, he didn't tell me."

"What's going to happen now?"

"They'll make a decision on whether they think Azure will come back or not. If they decide he's not, they'll probably throw us all out."

"Even though this is your home?"

"It's only my home because Azure was here. I'm nothing to them."

Erina's nose wrinkles in thought at his words to her brother. "Something I don't get is why Azure is in charge here since now it's pretty obvious he is. Everyone is so much older, why do they defer to him?"

Ocher shrugs, "He helped overthrow the previous leader, I guess they respect him."

"There are very few details on how that happened. Almost overnight we had a new mystery leader and the laws were relaxed. No one really knew what was going on or what happened to the guy before."

"Maybe you can ask Azure if we ever see him again."

"Will he tell us?"

"Probably not. He doesn't even like you."

Eren blinks, "So honest..."

He's not sure why they're surprised anymore. His facade has long since crumbled and he knows they've seen through his lies by now. Maybe they want to hold onto him just as much as he wants to hold onto Azure, for whatever reason that is.

"Ocher," a deeper voice calls out to him and he turns to see Dominicus approaching him. He wants to be angry at Dominicus for pressuring him. It would be so easy to put all the blame on him, but realistically he knows that he chose to give in and he's just as much at fault.

"What?"

"They decided that Azure ran away rather than fight and they're keeping with their original plan to invade. Are you coming with us?"

"I'm not in the army anymore." He sees the gazes of both twins snap to him in surprise. Lie after lie being revealed.

"I know," Dominicus agrees. "But you've also been that way and training is training. If they're as strong as Azure thinks, we'll need every soldier we have."

"Okay."

"Alright, get ready. The first group of us leave tomorrow morning."

Ocher nods, it's not like he has anything left here.

AZURE

"So, what's the plan?" Basel questions. "You've brought us this far, so tell me you have one."

He doesn't actually. He was more interested in leaving Haithen than figuring out a bunch of technicalities. Basel agreeing to come along was a surprise to him.

"I don't know." They dumped the truck in a thicket long before they reached the checkpoint on foot. He's hesitant to approach yet because they're already at a disadvantage and alerting guards to their presence will only make things worse.

What does he actually expect to be able to do against Vita's soldiers and the royal family? Not much. But he can still go out with a bang.

"Why the hell did you bring us back here then?"

"I didn't bring *us* back here, you chose to come with me."

"That's because I knew you were on some stupid suicide mission and I didn't want you to be alone!"

"I appreciate that, but now you can't complain."

Basel sighs, "This looks like the only road in, do you think the truck could make it through the forest without falling apart?"

"We can try? The worst that'll happen is we get stuck."

"And skipping the checkpoint to take them by surprise is the best."

"Fine," Azure agrees. "Let's head back."

They creep out of their hiding spot and head back the way they came on the empty road. The truck is right where they hid it and Basel hops in the driver's seat. "Can't have you dying midway, then killing me in a crash."

"It's your turn to drive anyway," Azure replies.

Basel puts the vehicle in drive and heads into the forest, avoiding the biggest trees and driving through the smaller ones. Azure thinks running over splintered trees is likely to puncture one of their tires, but he'll let Basel reap his own consequences.

He gives the steering wheel a sharp jerk left after they've put some distance between themselves and the road, crashing through the undergrowth with no care for the noise they're making.

"And you were worried about *me* killing us," Azure mutters.

"Difference is I'm not in danger of dropping dead at any moment and I'm wearing a seat belt." He stares pointedly at Azure who clicks his seatbelt on with a heavy sigh.

When Basel deems them far enough from the checkpoint, he spins the steering wheel and hits the gas until they burst out from the tree line amidst a tangle of leaves and broken wood.

"Fuck!" Basel slams on the brakes and they skid to a stop, facing the barrels of at least twenty guns pointed at them and a barrier of large rocks blocking their way forward. "That wasn't there before."

"Guess they got prepared," Azure says, already sliding out of his seatbelt. "Think the truck can get through those rocks?"

"Hell no! Someone from last time must've told them what we were driving and they made sure we couldn't just break through whatever barrier they set up."

"Back into the forest?"

"You're okay with me running these people over?" Basel does a quick count of the men surrounding their vehicle. "There aren't too many."

"...It's your call. You're driving, I'm just the passenger."

"Real nice, Azure," he replies sarcastically.

Azure watches as they roll out a large gun and point it at the vehicle. He sucks in a breath. They can stay in the truck and try to make a break for it, running people over or leave the truck and make for cover.

He doesn't want to kill these people because he can tell from their blank expressions that they're all being controlled. They haven't done anything wrong within their own free will and they're not fighters. Most of them are still dressed in the regular clothes they were wearing when they were forced out here. It's unfortunate, but if he and Basel don't take them out first, it's their heads.

"Make your choice fast, they're not waiting."

Basel ducks as the first warning bullet pings off the windshield. "Alright, we're mowing them down."

"Too late," Azure observes as several men drop a strip covered in several inch tall spikes into place around them. "You waited too long."

"You weren't helping either!" Basel snaps. "It's not only my fault!"

Several more bullets ping off the windshield, barely leaving a dent. "You think we could wait them out? They'll run out of bullets eventually."

Azure looks to where the larger gun is being aimed at them, "We can't wait out that one."

"New plan!" Basel opens his door. "*You're* going to mow them down!"

He shoots Basel a withering look as the other boy jumps from the vehicle, then he does the same, hitting the ground at a roll as their truck goes up in flames. He gets back to his feet, using the smoke as a cover to get out of sight.

There's nowhere to hide and he backs up against the truck, feeling the hot metal through his shirt. Looks like Basel's plan it is.

He summons up the last of his strength and grabs control of the flames rising from their burning vehicle. His whole body twitches from the effort and he can feel his muscles tightening. Basel better be grateful and use the distraction to get away.

Almost all the flames are under his control when he feels his legs give out, followed by chills breaking out along his skin and numbness in his fingers. It's too much.

He lets go.

CHAPTER 17: OCHER

Every bump and ridge on the uneven ground jostles him as their vehicle speeds across the land in record time. Whoever's driving must have a death wish with the careless way they take curves and their unwillingness to use the brake.

Dominicus squeezes his hand and gives him a reassuring smile after he tenses at the next jolt. He doesn't even try to smile back, he was never one for false smiles. In general, Dominicus is gentler with him. His touches are soft and ask permission, unlike Azure's possessiveness that always took.

He's all about choices whereas Azure never was.

They've been warned about the wolves and their solution is to hit the mountain in daylight with enough vehicles to keep any aggressive animals at bay. There hasn't been more than five minute stops this entire trip, enough for them to have a quick few minutes to themselves and driver change, then they were back on the road.

His nerves kick back in as they head down the mountain and get closer to Vita. Dominicus must sense this because an arm is draped around his shoulders to pull him over and it makes him sad. It's nice to be cared for this way again, but also, he wants it to be Azure.

Ocher closes his eyes, willing himself to sleep. He wants this to be over with as soon as possible.

They reach the same tiny town at the foot of the mountain by nightfall and to his annoyance, they actually stop here. Their caravan of army vehicles kicks up dust and disturbs the night with their noise, making people peer out their windows for the source of the sounds.

Unfortunately, once again Ciaran greets them. Ciaran's eyes sweep over the assembled soldiers, disappointment shines in his eyes when he doesn't see the person they both seem to be missing.

His distaste for Ciaran grows stronger. Ciaran doesn't have the *right* to miss Azure, they barely know each other.

Ciaran's eyes linger on him in confusion and recognition, and he turns away, stepping behind Dominicus' broad form.

"Do you know the way to your capital?" One of the captains demands of him.

"Yes," he answers hesitantly, eyes flicking around each stoic face. "Why?"

"We want to speak to your leaders and hopefully avoid a war that Vita will lose."

"Oh, so you're here to free everyone in the capital?"

"And take over as well."

Ciaran glances back at his sleepy, quiet town and Ocher can tell he's thinking about the way he's been stuck here since his birth. "I'll lead you."

"No!" Ocher blurts out before he can stop himself and people turn to look at him. "He can't be trusted," Ocher defends himself. "He's turning on his country that easily? He could lead us anywhere."

Ciaran tilts his head, studying him curiously, and most likely seeing through his flimsy excuse. After all, he hadn't made a secret of his dislike for the other boy. "Do *you* remember the way?"

No, of course he doesn't. He was too busy forcing Azure to pay attention to him to follow their route.

"You know him, Ocher?" Dominicus asks.

"I guided them to the capital when they came the first time," Ciaran answers for him. "We all made it there with no problem."

"Then, it's settled." The captain says. "He's coming."

Ocher shoots Ciaran a dark look before returning to their truck and closing the door with force. He doesn't want Ciaran's presence hanging around to make him recall their first trip. Ciaran is another reminder that Azure's focus was so easily swayed from him. He ignores Dominicus's look of confusion once the other man joins him inside after the next part of their plan has been decided.

He doesn't owe anyone any explanations.

Dominicus reaches out a hand to him and he shifts away, pressing himself against the door. He frowns, "Ocher, he told me why you don't like him."

"He's probably wrong," he replies without looking away from the window.

"Azure liked him."

"Barely." People really do talk too much.

"Relationships end, Ocher. It's not the end of the world and you can't hold on to those feelings forever, they'll smother you."

"How would *you* know? You were in the army longer than I was."

Dominicus laughs, "There were a few of us that had relationships, Ocher. You were too busy wishing to be anywhere else to notice."

He finally looks at Dominicus, "Really?"

"*Yes,* some of us made friends and *more.* You chose to be so alone, so believe me when I tell you, a relationship ending hurts, but there will always be other people and other chances."

He's been full witness to the truth of that statement, however his issue is that he doesn't *want* anyone else. He wants the person who no longer wants him and that's what makes it hurt worse. Ciaran is someone Azure may actually want now, he doesn't need that reminder in his face.

"Okay I believe you." That doesn't mean he's going to get over it though.

"Good," Dominicus reaches out and squeezes his hand as the truck's engine starts up again. "I'll be here."

◆ ◆ ◆

Their line of vehicles reaches the barricade in record time thanks to the same reckless speed they've used the whole trip and instead of pausing to speak, they drive through at high speed, barely leaving enough time for the guards to get out of the way.

"Aren't we trying to surprise them?"

"Nah, Haithen has never been patient and cunning. Get in, attack, take over, that's what the plans essentially boil down to."

"Efficient."

He's jerked forward, only restrained by his seatbelt when the driver abruptly hits the brakes. Dominicus climbs out of the truck to see what the hold up is and lets out a low whistle.

Ocher sticks his head out and sucks in a sharp breath before stepping out to join him.

Laid out before them is the aftermath of a massacre on the city outskirts. Dead soldiers litter the ground, some burned and some just dead. Charred grass smolders across the area and the air is heavy with the scent of smoke and burned flesh.

It looks like Azure's work, but why would he come back here? Ocher's gaze flicks back to one of the vehicles. For Ciaran?

Couldn't be, he dismisses. If Azure didn't come this way, then the only other option is that the royal family is punishing their own people.

Someone shouts and points to a lone soldier, still alive and trying to get his ruined flesh into a river. Ocher strides forward to reach him before anyone else can and pulls his head back, "What happened here?"

The soldier's eyes widen and he shakes his head desperately, "Nothing that concerns you, outsider."

"So nothing happened and this many people are dead?"

"No information for enemies, I'm not stupid."

"Stupidly loyal." Without warning, Ocher shoves his head in the water, holding it there for a few brief seconds before pulling the struggling soldier back up. "Try again. What happened?"

"Nothing! A truck exploded!"

"All on its own?" The man averts his eyes and that's all he needs to see to shove his head back under.

"Ocher!" Dominicus' horrified shout cuts across the man's wild flailing. "What are you doing?"

"Getting answers."

"Not this way!" Dominicus attempts to pull him off, but Ocher shoves him away and glares.

"I'll stop when he speaks." His attention focuses back on the soldier and when he begins to go limp, Ocher pulls him back up. "I can do this all day."

"Wait," Dominicus says.

"I'll tell you," the man gasps out. "There was an outsider. His truck caught on fire and then it spread everywhere. It was endless."

"What?" Dominicus asks. "One truck and one person did all this?"

That definitely sounds like Azure. Ocher tosses the burned man aside. "Azure and Basel came this way." They can't be too far ahead of them considering their truck was destroyed and the city isn't on fire yet.

Dominicus looks at the scene again, "I guess I shouldn't be surprised he did this. He's still as destructive as ever."

"Maybe, sometimes people deserve it," Ocher mutters, yanking open the door, and climbing back inside. "Let's go!"

Dominicus reluctantly gets back in, shooting him more concerned looks that he continues to ignore. If Dominicus doesn't like what he chooses to do, that's his own issue.

Their caravan of vehicles drives farther in, slowly moving past the wreckage and the dead. They come to another stop and a few soldiers hop out to clear spike strips that have been placed in their path.

Ocher scans the area for any more survivors and catches sight of a motionless lump facedown in the grass next to the road and Ocher would recognize him anywhere. "Azure!" He runs over and drops to his knees to flip Azure's still body over. He's awake, but his eyes are glassy and he takes short, shallow breaths.

Dominicus crouches down next to him with Ciaran only a step behind. "So, you were right, he really did come here. Is he okay?"

"I'm not sure. Azure?" He reaches out to shake his shoulder, "Can you hear me?"

He squints up in confusion, awareness slowly coming back into his eyes. Azure's gaze lands on him first, then slides to Dominicus and Ocher's hand is abruptly slapped away. "Don't touch me."

Ocher pulls back in hurt and surprise, even though he shouldn't have expected anything else. If Azure wanted him around, he wouldn't have left without a word.

Azure pulls himself upright, "Where's Basel?"

"I don't see him. Why did you leave?"

He glances at Dominicus again, "You don't get to ask me questions." Azure pushes him aside and gets shakily to his feet, "I need to find Basel."

Ciaran stares up in concern, "Azure, are you okay?"

The way his gaze softens on Ciaran is noticeable and Ocher is struck with the urge to knock Ciaran over and bury his face in the ground until he suffocates.

Azure pulls him up, "I'm fine. Help me look?"

"Okay," Ciaran says.

Dominicus touches his stiff shoulders in reassurance as they stumble away together, "Ocher, it's fine. This is part of moving on."

It is *not* fine. He doesn't *want* to move on, why doesn't Dominicus understand that? He keeps trying to reassure him, but this situation is still his fault for pressuring him and 'being there' for him won't help anything.

There wouldn't be any moving on if Dominicus hadn't kissed him. Ocher pulls away and heads towards a different vehicle, suddenly he can't stand the sight of Dominicus anymore.

CHAPTER 18: AZURE

Ciaran is there with him as he searches for Basel. He knows Basel wouldn't have gone far alone, so he doesn't understand why it's taking so long to find him. He's exhausted. It's getting bad. Dark spots flicker across his vision and his leg is numb, he can barely feel it as he walks.

Worst of all is Ciaran's energy calling to him so strongly, his body is begging for him to take it.

Haithen is so stupid, they shouldn't have come here. He warned them and they came anyway. Vita will have them shooting each other, then they'll subjugate everyone left alive. Even that annoying betrayer will probably get himself killed because when he dies, Ocher becomes more vulnerable.

"Azure." The voice comes from somewhere to his left and he hadn't even realized that Basel had found them. Hands take hold of his shoulders and gently lower him to the ground. "This is the end, huh?"

"...Yeah." He barely has the energy to look up into Basel's worried hazel eyes. His face swims across his vision and he'd be nauseous if he was still capable of it.

"He's dying?" Ciaran asks.

Basel stares down at him, "Yes." He looks around and Azure knows what he's thinking. Their truck is destroyed and he's stuck in this country. Basel probably knows his chances of making it back home are slim.

Haithen is here, but Basel has seen this country in action too, he knows they won't offer much protection. His best chance is to steal one of the army's vehicles and make a break for it. Azure lets his eyes drift shut, he wonders what Basel will choose. He's a survivalist at heart.

"Azure," Basel jostles him back to attention. "I can't die here."

"Then you better get running."

"No, seriously. I'm too young to die, and rich. It'll all go to waste."

Azure laughs tiredly. "That's what you care about?"

"I happen to love my life, thank you very much. Unlike you who's willing to give up and die."

"It's not like I have a choice."

"Except you do." He inhales sharply. Basel would really ask that of him right now? "You could ensure both of us got back."

"And what's there for me? Ruling some dumb country?"

"Then take your money and leave!"

"And go where? Run around alone and miserable?"

"I'll go with you!"

He huffs out a quiet sound, "I thought you were trying to convince me."

"Do it for your spoiled little asshole then."

Azure is quiet. Ocher will die here too. In fact, if Haithen loses, Vita might unite them all under one country with only Meio escaping unscathed. It's not something he cares to think about at this point.

Sure, it would be better if Ocher survived, but he'd still be gone and they wouldn't be together, so what's it really matter? Honestly, he's not sure how much longer Ocher would live once he's gone. Then again, maybe he's underestimating him. He's proven he can and will survive alone.

His feelings on Ocher are...complicated. In the beginning, he'd resisted him because he could tell even back then that Ocher was the type that it would be near impossible to get rid of, whether through sheer stubbornness or genuine affection, Ocher wouldn't let go.

He was repressed and desperate, lonely enough that when Azure came along, there was almost nothing to stop him from trying to get involved. Every sneaky touch and his desire to stay close, Ocher was so easy to peel open and influence. But, he had wanted to keep him at a distance, unwilling to emotionally involve himself with someone else, especially without knowing if he could trust them.

Azure had tested him so many times and never in a kind way. Ocher had been pushed and pushed, manipulated and forced into doing things he didn't necessarily want to do. He knows that he was never the nicest to the younger male, but in the end, Ocher still chose to stay with him, so he let his guard down and let him in as much as he was willing.

They'd spent a year in perfect happiness and if he spent that time unraveling every bit of independence Ocher had gained and making sure he never wanted to leave him, who cared? It worked for them.

And then, Ocher had left him anyway and everything he'd done had been worthless. There were no more touches between them, no more waking up to Ocher having crawled into his bed in the middle of the night, no gray eyes locked on him all the time, and no one for him to care for. After that, he'd been forced to admit to himself just how much he wanted Ocher and he hated that weakness, it's what he'd spent his life trying to avoid.

Finding out he was dying wasn't a curse, there was nothing holding him here. The only thing he wanted was to make sure he saw Ocher one last time, he hadn't meant to get that close to him all over again. He just keeps making mistakes now.

"You know, I really did love him," Azure says.

"I know you did. We *all* know you did. So why don't you live so you can tell him?"

Azure shakes his head weakly, the movement barely noticeable. "If I can't have all of him, I don't want him."

"Who's stopping you?" Basel demands. "I promise he'd come running back to you with open arms."

"He kissed Dominicus."

"He was probably confused and that's *your* fault for constantly refusing him!"

Azure closes his eyes, that's a nice thought.

"Azure!" Basel smacks him and Ciaran makes a sound of protest. "I don't even like the annoying guy, but I know he loves you back and would sacrifice whatever you wanted to make you happy. Get up and fix things! It's not too late."

"And if it is? I won't live for nothing."

"Then die afterwards. In fact, I'll help you. I'll give you a grand funeral where everyone celebrates your death, but make sure you aren't leaving anything unfinished."

He's quiet, considering Basel's words. Is his own happiness worth someone else's life? Yes, he's killed before to get what he wanted, but not someone so completely innocent. Then again, it's not just his life. It's his, Ocher's, Basel's, the soldiers that came from Haithen, and anyone else who might die if Vita wins.

One life versus all those. It would be easier if he had no care for that one life.

Azure sucks in a deep breath. He's going to have to live with all of this. This better be worth it. "I'm taking you down with me if everything still falls apart," he tells Basel.

"Sure, if I don't slip something in your food the minute it looks like things might go sideways."

He gives a faint laugh, he's pretty sure Basel isn't joking. Azure reaches out a shaky hand, "Ciaran?" He calls softly and he hates knowing that the other boy doesn't suspect anything when he takes hold of his hand.

Azure squeezes his hand gently, he won't make this painful.

Afterwards, he rests Ciaran's limp body on the ground and hates himself for getting into this position. He hates both responsibility and regrets.

"Is he dead?" Basel murmurs, peering over his shoulder.

"Yes, I should never have come here."

"Haithen would have come here anyway, then they all might have died."

"Who cares? I would've already been dead, it wouldn't have mattered to me. Now, I have to live with this." He gives Basel a hard shove to the ground.

"Hey!" Basel protests. "Don't take it out on me! Don't tell me you actually feel guilty? That's a change."

"What's that supposed to mean? I do have a heart."

"You have a heart mostly when it comes to Ocher," Basel corrects. "Everyone else is collateral."

"Shut up."

"You're just mad because you can't do what you want anymore. Now, there's consequences for the things you do."

"Still going to do what I want."

Basel grabs his hand and hoists him up. "I'm sorry you had to do that, but if we make it through this, you can lock yourself away with Ocher and do all the 'making up' you want. He won't complain."

Azure wrinkles his nose, "Let's not go that far."

CHAPTER 19: OCHER

It's tense in the truck as they leave the first area scattered with bodies and head closer to the city, unaware of what to expect.

Surprisingly, Azure and Basel had returned to join them. Unsurprisingly, they had picked a different vehicle to ride in and Azure hadn't looked his way once. He wants to talk to him again, but it's clear finding Azure hasn't changed anything.

They begin to slow as the capital comes into view. The streets are empty except for row after row of civilian soldiers standing in perfect lines, blocking their path forward.

Ocher leans forward, "Are we going to drive through them too?"

The driver's hands tighten around the steering wheel, "Not sure. It would probably be easier than fighting."

"Where's the base?"

Ocher points to the bronze tower near the center, "There. That's where the royal family lives."

"Harder to get there on foot."

They're at a standoff, waiting for Vita to make a move or their lead captain to make a decision. He almost misses the brief flash of silver as something rolls from behind enemy lines to disappear under the first truck.

As one, the civilian soldiers step back in perfect synchronization to avoid the explosion as the truck goes up in flames. His eyes widen in surprise as the driver shifts into reverse and he's thrown forward. Dominicus steadies him, staring forward with shell shocked brown eyes and everyone else had the same idea because their truck rams another one almost immediately.

The screech of metal scraping against metal makes him wince and he realizes they're not getting out of here anytime soon. A second truck explodes and they're still trapped in a bottleneck. Once the third is blown up, he's done waiting for their turn.

Ocher climbs over the seat and falls into the trunk area, quickly unlatching it and shimmying over the truck crushed against theirs. By this time, others have realized they'll be killed if they stay locked in their vehicles and doors start opening.

The minute some of them step out and drop to their knees behind the doors for protection, Vita opens an avalanche of fire. Ocher keeps low to the ground, using the entire truck as a shield.

A few feet from him, a soldier falls and Haithen is either pathetic or they've never actually had someone challenge them because they're scrambling. Some return fire, but from his spot, Ocher can see that Vita is so well organized that it's ineffective.

The first few lines all hold shields to protect those behind them and the remaining soldiers fire over their shoulders. Haithen must have conquered countries based on sheer numbers and the luck of their victims being unprepared.

Vita is in a perfect formation and when one of Haithen's trucks breaks free from the wreckage and accelerates towards them instead of away, they part in a perfect wave. Not a single person fires on the truck, but it doesn't get far either before it's gone in a burst of wreckage too.

This is getting worse and worse. He can see more trucks from the back of their caravan arriving, but they're blocked from going any further by the bottleneck, not that they would be much help anyway if everyone has been trained the same.

They should have gone for a surprise attack. Where is he supposed to go now? Retreat? Try to get past them until he's shot by a random person in the streets?

Ocher peeks around the side and there's no change in the lines, they're facing an impenetrable wall of men. He readjusts his sweaty grip on his gun and pulls back to shelter. It's so hot now, sweat drips into his eyes and irritates them even more than all the smoke filling the air.

Dominicus and the other two who were with them don't look much better, they're crouched in the back exchanging wide eyed looks of fear with each other.

There's another shout from further back and several men come running towards the front. Ocher looks back to see flames from some of the wrecked trucks growing stronger, coalescing into a single sweltering wall of blaze that sweeps across the enemy soldiers.

He breathes a sigh of relief. Azure has decided to help them.

Vita's formation falls apart as they try to escape the unnatural wall of fire and Haithen wastes no time in advancing, shooting as they charge. Ocher follows behind them, maiming stragglers, but unwilling to be on the front lines.

This is his first real experience with war. Ironically enough, he saw more violence outside of the army than when he was actually part of it. Ocher weaves through the fallen bodies, looking into the glassy and unseeing eyes of a few.

None of them attempt to dodge Haithen's bullets with any amount of fluidity, just jerky movements. They seem incapable of moving independently and that only helps Haithen.

Ocher catches a glimpse of Dominicus breaking someone's arm to keep them from shooting and he fires at another one. There's so many of Vita's citizens here and they don't even react when one of them is hit. They simply step over, or on them, and keep moving.

A sting in his side leaves him wincing and he looks down to see crimson spreading across his shirt. He presses his hand against the wound. It's painful, but nowhere near as painful as the time Azure set him on fire from the inside, still hurts though.

With his slower movements now, he's near useless and an easy target. They won't miss him if he bows out. This isn't worth his life.

AZURE

Once he and Basel join one of the vehicles in the caravan, the line of vehicles continues forward. They're near the middle, so when the first truck is targeted, they're far enough away that their vehicle is barely impacted by the explosion.

He leans across the front seat to get a better view of what's happening and falls headfirst when their vehicle is abruptly smashed into. Basel laughs, making no effort to pull him upright.

The soldiers in the front seat lift him up and Basel yanks him the rest of the way back by his shirt. "I think that was one of the most awkward things I've seen you do and I see you more than most people."

"I *fell*."

"I know and I've never seen you fall so terribly."

"I did just recover from nearly dying," Azure reminds him.

The ground shakes from the aftermath of a second explosion and shrapnel bounces off their windshield. The vehicle in front reverses backwards, smashing into them without a second thought and Azure sighs, now they're well and truly stuck.

"Should we get out?" Basel suggests.

"I'll get out and deal with this. You stay."

Azure stands beside the truck, coaxing the smoldering remnants of the destroyed vehicles back to full strength. From there, it's easy to sweep those flames up into something destructive enough to take out Vita's formation in one hit, clearing the way for Haithen's forces to break through.

As the fighting moves inward, he remains near the back, moving at a leisurely pace. Unless something gets set on fire, he's not much help on the front lines. He's not going to overexert himself trying to drag the fire the whole way or continuously coax flames from almost nothing. He's learned his lesson on that.

Haithen has the advantage now, all they need to do is finish this, and they can all go home. It's obvious all these people are being controlled. Vita's soldiers can't take individual action, so if Haithen manages to throw some type of plan together that requires multiple decisions to counter, they should be able to overpower them.

He wonders if Vita's soldiers can still feel while their bodies are under someone else's control or if their awareness is too far gone. This is why his people never dabbled in this, it was too cruel for most to have the power to force people to throw away their lives while they were helpless inside their own bodies. Free will is something they strongly believed in.

Their group reaches the tower and fans out to surround it, fighting the few of Vita's forces remaining. Azure moves away from the fighting, content to watch from a distance. He's not a soldier and never had any desire to become one.

His eyes slip shut as a tremor runs through him, leaving him cold and shaking. Apparently he's not fully recovered yet. Azure intends to melt away into one of the alleys to rest, but instead, his throat comes to rest right against the sharp blade of a knife.

"Eulysia," he guesses.

"This is your fault," she hisses into his ear. "You never should have come here."

"And you wouldn't have eventually tried to take over Haithen?"

"Now you'll never know," she presses the knife into his skin, leaving the faintest cut against his throat. "If I could force you to kill yourself, I would. But, I take it you're related to the people from Meio."

Azure makes a noncommittal noise, she doesn't need to know anything about him.

Eulysia takes it as an affirmation anyway. "Tell them to fall back."

"I don't control them," he replies. "I can't force them all back like you do your people."

"I know that, but after your visit, it was obvious that you're someone important in Haithen with enough power to stop this. They won't want to risk your life."

Azure laughs shortly. Haithen's leadership would probably be thrilled if he turned up dead in Vita. "They won't care."

"Then I have no reason not to kill you if you're that worthless."

Her arm shakes the barest amount and he feels the sharp edge cutting a deeper rift into his skin. If she's going to do this, she should at least be fast about it.

The knife digs in deeper and she shouts abruptly, falling away as the knife scrapes down his neck. Azure steps quickly away and turns to see Dominicus pinning her down. "This is a surprise."

"Why? Because you would have let her kill me?"

"Maybe."

"I'm not you," Dominicus says.

"I think everyone would agree that one of me is enough."

"*More* than enough," Dominicus agrees.

Azure can see from the way Eulysia's eyes lock on Dominicus that she's about to attempt control over him and Azure reaches out a hand to his shoulder, blocking her with a light touch. Dominicus blinks at him, startled, and Azure gets it. He's never willingly come close to Dominicus, let alone touched him. It's only for self preservation, but Dominicus wouldn't know that.

Eulysia glares daggers at him and Azure stares her in the eye when he orders, "Cuff her." Dominicus obeys and stands, staring at him expectantly and Azure frowns, "I won't say thank you for saving me."

"Fine. I didn't do it for you anyway. I did it for Ocher, only because I don't think he'll ever let you go."

"Good, then keep your mouth off him."

Dominicus smirks, "We'll see."

Azure glares. If he has to add another person to share a cell with Ocher's brothers, he won't hesitate.

Eulysia shifts and his focus switches back to her. "I'm sure the rest of your family will join you soon enough," he tells her.

"My parents are far stronger than me!"

"Sure." Now, what to do with her? They can't keep guards on her when she can influence them to free her at any moment. "Hmm."

A wicked smile crosses his face. The best way to ensure she can't free herself is to make her powerless. He's rarely greedy, but he'll make an exception this time. Azure drops down in front of her, reaches out two hands to brush her hair back, and *drains.*

It's a rush, far more than he received from Ciaran. Her energy is much stronger than Ciaran's. It fills in all the gaps in his own fractured body and more, giving him enough to fully counter the effects of the amplifier for at least a few years more.

"I feel better than I have in ages," he says once he's done and he can feel the extra energy circulating through his body and reinvigorating him.

Dominicus looks down to where Eulysia is curled in on herself, sobbing. "What did you do to her?"

"Nothing, you should put her away somewhere, she won't be hurting anyone else."

Dominicus gives him another suspicious look, but drags her away to a higher ranking captain. They'll decide where to hold her and what to do.

Meanwhile, anyone remaining from Vita has dropped their weapons. They have no will to fight and without being controlled, no reason to. All of them surrender, begging to be allowed to return home. Despite the protests, he allows it. They're no threat.

Eulysia's been taken care of, but her mother and father are still running free. He can only assume they're nowhere nearby since free will was returned to Vita's citizens. Half of Haithen's remaining forces are guarding the exits and the other half are searching the tower, however Basel's nowhere to be found in all the unfamiliar faces.

Azure grabs the closest soldier, "Where's Basel?"

"I don't know," he answers. "He ran off a while ago, I think."

Well, Basel could be anywhere by now, maybe even in someone's home having a meal until all this is over. No point wasting his energy searching for him. However he can feel which direction Ocher is, and that's much easier to follow.

CHAPTER 20: OCHER

He's resigned himself to leaning against this tree and pretending to be dead in the hopes that everyone will overlook him when Basel arrives and starts shaking him. "Hey, you dead?"

"Not yet," he answers, aware of the blood seeping between his fingers. "What are you doing here?"

"I could ask you the same."

"You never come near anything dangerous. You make it a point to stay far away."

"Yeah well, Azure's my friend." He shrugs. "Don't make that face. He is. I just didn't know it would turn out like this. Anyway, come on."

"Where are we going?"

"Leave the soldiers to fight each other, we care about the royals."

Ocher lets his head drop back against the tree in annoyance. "And what exactly are we supposed to do against them?"

"Well, me? Nothing. They might have me kill myself. You, on the other hand, can resist better, so it's on you."

He looks down at his bleeding side, "I don't think I'm going anywhere right now."

"You'll be fine," Basel dimisses. He takes off his jacket and lifts up Ocher's shirt to tighten his jacket around the wound. "See? A perfect tourniquet."

Ocher looks at the wrapping skeptically, "Right."

"Move, we're sitting ducks here."

"Where's Azure?"

Basel makes an impatient noise, "Don't worry about him, worry about yourself."

Ocher lets himself be pulled into the center of Haithen's defenses, using the others for protection as they move further into the city. The streets remain empty of citizens as they pass through. Everyone was probably evacuated and if not, they're in hiding.

Haithen continues to fight the people stationed at various points in their path to the tower, but the farther they get from the destroyed trucks, the less fire there is and soon enough Basel ducks away from the group, pulling him along as the rest approach the tower.

"They have more guards here, they must be inside."

"How are we going to find them through all those floors even if we do manage to get inside?" Ocher questions.

"We don't need to get inside," Basel answers. "We smoke them out, they can't stay in there forever."

Dominicus reaches them and fixes Basel with a look, "You're a civilian, you shouldn't be here."

"Then make sure I get back home safe."

"I'm not responsible for civilians who throw themselves into danger. Ocher," Dominicus' eyes widen when he finally sees his bloody shirt and the jacket roughly tied around him. "Are you okay?" Dominicus reaches for him and he pushes his hand aside.

"I'm fine," Ocher answers, looking back to the tower and pulling their attention back to what matters. "You really think they'll run out to face us?"

"Or die," Basel says. "Oh, that's not good. He immediately steps away, putting distance between himself and them.

"What is it?" Dominicus turns back to their soldiers, but Vita is still outnumbered.

"I think they've taken control of Haithen." As if to confirm Basel's words, several of Haithen's soldiers begin firing on each other. "Yep, they've definitely taken control. Can't say we didn't predict that."

"I didn't!" Dominicus exclaims.

"Azure is selective with information."

"Tell me about it," Ocher mutters. Selective with information is a nice way to put it.

Dominicus shoots Basel another dirty look and runs back towards his comrades, doing his best to stop them from shooting each other.

"He shouldn't do that, he's going to get himself killed too. You should -" Basel cuts off and turns to the right, scanning the area quickly.

"What?"

"I saw something, let's go. I think they made a break for it while Haithen was distracted."

Ocher runs after Basel, ignoring the continuous pain in his side. It had lessened some, but it flares back up as he runs, forcing him to slow down into a jog. "Should we be chasing them alone?"

"They'll be too busy controlling the soldiers," Basel shouts back to him. "Shoot that guy on your left!"

He turns to see one of Vita's men approaching them and he fires. "Why couldn't you?"

"Because I only have two shots left and I'm saving them!"

Perfect. Ocher follows Basel through the streets, following after something only he can see. He occasionally catches a glimpse of color as someone disappears around a corner. It doesn't seem like whoever it is explored the city much and he and Basel are much faster than people who have lived their entire lives sheltered inside a tower, so they gain on them quickly enough.

They're being led farther away, but there doesn't seem to be a goal in mind, just escape. King Vin and Queen Euna come fully into sight and Basel fires, hitting King Vin in the leg and crippling him. Queen Euna turns in a fury and Basel goes rigid.

Shit. They're too far for them to keep their control of the soldiers, now her full focus is on them.

Basel looks at him and Ocher thinks he almost looks apologetic before putting a bullet in his leg as well. He crumbles and King Vin springs on him, wrapping hands around his throat while Queen Euna keeps Basel under control.

His gun is knocked far from his hand and he struggles to push King Vin off him, but he's bigger and not hampered by being shot twice. Way to be useless, Basel, Ocher thinks as he manages to get his forearm under the King's neck and pushes.

He hears the click of Basel's empty gun and allows a small moment of relief that the last bullet went into his leg.

"Hurry! Kill him, we have to go!" Queen Euna shouts.

"I'm trying!" King Vin yells back and Ocher can feel the prodding in his mind now that he knows what to watch out for.

Basel advances towards them, ready to bring the gun down on his head and when he comes within arm's reach, Ocher lets King Vin's hands tighten around his throat to swing his arm out and grab Basel's ankle. He falls forward over them and Ocher snatches his gun before he can recover and slams it down on King Vin's head.

The King collapses heavily on top of him, adding to Basel's weight and knocking the wind out of him. He barely has a second to try and squirm free before Queen Euna's furious shriek is echoing through the area and then there's a piercing pain in his head. All thoughts of controlling him are gone, she's after revenge. The pain in his head spreads, cutting through his mind and blocking out anything other than the sensation of his mind being painfully ripped apart.

He must pass out for a few moments because the next thing he's aware of is Queen Euna on the ground and Basel has his gun in one hand and is shaking him with the other. Ocher sits up and blood drips from his nose, leaving the tang of iron on his lips.

Basel helps him push King Vin's unconscious body off and roll him to the side. "She almost got you and he's not even dead." Queen Euna's arm hangs limply at her side and blood trickles from her fingers to pool on the ground. "I guess pain makes it hard to concentrate, but just in case," Basel crosses over to her in a few quick steps and brings Ocher's gun down to knock her unconscious too. "Finally this shit is over."

"What about Eulysia?"

"I'm sure the others will take care of her, if they're not too incompetent. Get up."

"We just leave them here?"

"If we move fast, we can tell someone and they can come back and get them before they wake up," Basel explains.

Ocher gestures to his leg and side, "I can't move fast like this."

"Good point." Basel squats down and helps him onto his back. When Basel stands, carrying him as well, Ocher's surprised. Basel is stronger than he thought, but he's also confused as to why Basel's being so nice for once. It wouldn't be out of character for Basel to just leave him here until someone else came to find them.

As Basel starts heading back towards the center of the city, he doesn't ask. He's not sure he wants to know the answer.

They walk in the direction of shouting and noise, there's less sounds of gunfire, so maybe Basel's right and everything has been taken care of. He hopes so because he's *tired.*

"You know, you could probably wear Azure down if you tried hard enough," Basel says. "Actually," he pauses. "You might not have to try that hard."

Ocher scoffs, "He's made it clear that he wants nothing to do with me."

"Don't be so sure." Basel hefts him up higher to keep him from slipping, "He still likes you."

"Azure hates me. That whole trip, bringing me along? It was just an excuse to make me miserable and remind me of how badly I messed up."

"Trust me when I say he doesn't hate you. He wants to dote on you just as much as you like him to dote on you. Just stop screwing up."

"Should you be telling me this?"

"Why? Because I'm supposed to think of you as competition for Azure?"

"...Yes." That's exactly it.

Basel laughs. "Despite what you think, I have *no* interest in dating Azure. He's a little too mean, or maybe rude? Controlling? Stubborn? I don't know, but he's too much of a prick for me."

This makes no sense, Basel has always made his interest obvious. "Then why did you always make comments like that!"

"Because it bothered you," he answers easily. "And you made it way too easy to rile you up. It was funny and Azure wasn't doing anything about it."

"It wasn't funny."

"Not to you, it wasn't, but you also have no sense of humor."

"I do!"

"When was the last time you laughed?" Hm..he can't really remember, probably some time during the past year, definitely before that he knows, but after? It's a mystery. "That's what I thought," Basel says with satisfaction. "I barely ever see you smile."

"Maybe I don't want to smile at you."

"Oh that's right, you save that for Dominicus."

Ocher pauses, "He told you."

"Of course. But like I said, he doesn't hate you. He'll come around."

"Hm."

The silhouette of someone approaching them appears as they get closer and Basel tenses beneath him. He prays it's not an enemy, he can't run and Basel can't run while carrying him at the same time.

Basel stops, letting the person approach them first. Azure comes into view and both of them sag in relief. Despite everything, he's still *so* happy to see him.

Azure stops in front of him and his eyes sweep over the two of them, "Unscathed as always, Basel."

"Yep."

A long look passes between them, one that he's not privy to, but it ends with a shake of Azure's head, and then Azure's reaching out to him. To his shock, he's transferred from Basel to Azure's back. His arms automatically go around Azure's neck as the other boy holds him securely by the thighs.

Basel rolls out his shoulders, "Much better." He leads the way back and the two of them fill each other in, neither of them acknowledging him again. It's almost like he's not even here with them.

Azure's hair is loose, coming undone from his braid and Ocher presses his face into it, inhaling his familiar scent overlaid with a mix of sweat and the smell of burning metal. He's prepared to be dropped for crossing boundaries, but surprisingly Azure's grip tightens instead. Was Basel right?

They reach the remainder of Haithen's forces and Basel tells a captain where the King and Queen were left and some men hurry to capture them before they wake. Azure drops him off at a hastily constructed first aid area, barely looking at him as the workers help him from Azure's back and lay him flat to slowly untie Basel's jacket from his wound.

He just wants Azure to *look* at him again, to acknowledge that he exists. "Wait," he calls before Azure can walk away.

"Let them patch you up, you'll be fine tomorrow," he responds dismissively.

Ocher drops his head back in resignation. He might be fine tomorrow, but will they?

CHAPTER 21: AZURE

Finding Ocher is easy. Following the pull of him from the tower and into the north side of the city brought him straight towards the other boy. The streets are deserted and he has no idea why Ocher would have come this way. There's no one here and nowhere to go.

He gets the answer to his question when both Basel and Ocher come into view. He's honestly surprised to see the two of them together and getting along. Ocher is clearly injured, but as usual, Basel is unharmed.

Basel gives him a look that heavily implies he should be grateful that Basel is trying to keep his word that life is still worth living by bringing Ocher back. He supposes he can appreciate the effort since it is Basel's fault that he's still alive.

He reaches out and Ocher is swapped onto his back easily. There's still a lot there that he doesn't feel like thinking about right now, so for the moment, he's content to ignore the less immediate problem.

Basel tells him what happened and where they left the King and Queen. After they're picked up, he may go drain them as well. It will ensure that the worst threat is completely resolved.

He's unfortunately not dead, so when he returns to Haithen, that will make one less thing he has to worry about. Maybe he'll abdicate, but he really does like the mansion and all the perks.

Ocher's pressing against him and he can feel the weight of all the words the other boy wants to say in his silence, but he's really not in the mood to have that conversation, and as much as he loves Basel, he doesn't want to have the conversation in front of him either. He's carrying Ocher and that should be enough for him.

Once they reach the roughly constructed first aid area, he dumps Ocher off to be tended to. He'll heal fast enough. Ocher probably hasn't noticed, but a normal person would be unconscious, or at least fatally wounded after taking two shots like he did. He's still conscious, talking, and nowhere close to passing out from the pain.

The captains are discussing everything that's happened so far and how they'll move forward. It's a serious discussion, but he can't help being amused by the way Dominicus' mouth hangs open in shock as someone explains to him the full extent of the royal family's abilities.

Dominicus regards him suspiciously when he notices his arrival. "So, you can do those things too?"

Hm, the secret's out. "Maybe, guess that means I've shown you mercy."

"Oh yeah?" He raises an eyebrow. "Or maybe you just didn't want Ocher angry at you."

"We're not together right now and it's been a long day, don't push your luck."

He laughs, "Fine. What happens now?"

"Well, I'm not taking war prisoners, so I say leave them here for the citizens to deal with as they see fit. They can get their come-uppance and the citizens can decide how harsh it is. After all, they're the ones who suffered the most."

"And the others?"

"The others will have to be hunted down, preferably by Vita's citizens rather than us. Everyone's aware of what they can do now, they'll be prepared. The other members of the royal family stationed in different areas may go into hiding themselves, but I don't think they'll try to fill in the gap."

"So, we'll just leave them to fend for themselves?" Dominicus asks skeptically.

Azure pauses. Actually, maybe that wouldn't be for the best. The threat has been taken care of, but these people have been under their control for a long time. It might make the situation worse to have every leader in the country gone at once.

"On second thought, when I get back, I'll kick out a few advisors who have annoyed me and tell them to come help maintain order. They forced me to come here, it's only fair they see it through to the end."

"They won't want to do that."

Azure smiles, "They won't have a choice. I'm in charge and as much as they might hate it, I'm not dead either." Dominicus makes a complicated expression at his words, opening his mouth to say something and then seeming to think better of it. "Spit out whatever you want to say."

He hesitates, taking a few steps back to put more space between them. "Did you control Ocher like that to keep him with you for so long? The minute you let him go, he left."

Ah, this bastard. How dare he think he knows anything about their relationship. Now he's done being civil. Azure gives him a tight smile, "If I did, do you really think I would admit it?"

Azure moves away as the truck that retrieved the King and Queen arrives back and everyone gives it a wide berth. He walks over to peer inside. They're still unconscious and thrown haphazardly in the trunk. That makes this slightly easier for them.

He places a hand on each of their hands, feels the energy of their power and he's almost apologetic. He'd hate it if he woke up powerless one day. Then again, he's not the one subjugating the will of an entire country.

Azure pulls, filling his body with their spirit until they're empty, but still living. Even for him, it's too much. He feels another twinge of regret for Ciaran. If only he had made it here first. They could withstand this. Ciaran didn't have enough energy for his body to withstand what he needed to take.

Stepping back, Azure shuts the trunk on them and this whole venture. Everyone is safe now. Basel can live out his life like he wanted. He glances around and no one is preparing to depart, so he looks up at the tower and it doesn't look too damaged. It would be a good place to sleep.

Azure doesn't get within a few steps of the tower's entrance before there's a hesitant hand on his arm. He knows who it is already, can recognize him from the faintest touch. The pull also helps.

He turns and gray eyes look into his own. Azure closes his eyes for a brief second and lets out a deep exhale, "What is it, Ocher?"

The fingers on his arm tighten minutely, and he doesn't say what he really wants. Instead, Ocher glances over his shoulder. "Where's Ciaran?"

Why the hell does he care? He's been insanely, and unnecessarily, jealous of him since the beginning. "Not here."

"What happened to him?"

Basel approaches, but pulls back to wait when he sees them talking. "He won't be around anymore," Azure answers, ignoring the way Basel's eyes widen in surprise.

"What's that mean?"

"It means he's dead," he explains bluntly.

Ocher pulls back, "Did you kill him?" Does he really have to answer that? This isn't the conversation he thought he'd be having right now. "You did," Ocher assumes when he gets no answer.

"It was an accident."

"How do you accidentally kill someone?" He shouts. "He liked you!"

"You left me," Azure says, waiting for the impact of his words to register. "It made me weak since you hold a part of me. I needed something to fill it."

"Oh," he says faintly, hunching in on himself. "Why didn't you bring me back sooner?"

"I didn't want to force you back if you didn't want to come. You wanted freedom and you chose to leave. I wasn't going to take that from you."

"So, it's my fault." Ocher stares at the ground, hiding his face, and Azure can feel the guilt and confusion rolling off him.

It makes him feel guilty too. It wasn't Ocher's fault, and he's tired of being angry at Ocher for leaving him. He's tired of a lot of things actually. "It's not your fault. Ciaran was at the wrong place at the wrong time. You're your own person, you have no obligation to stay and you still don't. What I do shouldn't concern you."

He means for the words to be reassuring, to be taken neutrally, but Ocher flinches back from him, expression shuttering as he looks away and he's too tired to figure out what's wrong now. Dominicus approaches them and he steps away, continuing his walk to the entrance. He's definitely not up for dealing with both of them at the same time.

Basel falls into step with him. "You're not going to tell him the truth?"

"What good would that do? What good does telling him anything do?"

"Azure, don't be difficult," Basel chides.

"I'm not! You think knowing everything would change his decisions? It won't! I'm sick of all this, these people, this place! I just want to be back home and through with everyone."

"You're tired," Basel observes.

"Probably," he admits. The past few days are catching up to him and for once, he's dealing with emotions worse than Ocher does.

"I'm not saying tell him everything, but you should at least talk to him. Like I said, he's still willing, *more* than willing. And I want to know sooner rather than later if I need to plan your funeral."

"Yeah," he laughs mirthlessly. "Wouldn't want you to miss out on keeping your word."

Basel glances up as they stop in front of the tower doors, "Are you sleeping here?"

"Yes, so don't bother me unless we're leaving. Take care of every-thing else, *advisor.*"

Azure heads upstairs to the room where he stayed previously and finds it neatly prepared, just like the last time he stayed here. He collapses in exhaustion, ignoring how sooty and dirty he is. It feels like this day has lasted forever.

CHAPTER 22: OCHER

A young child runs up to him and hands off another item of food, pie this time, before running back the way she came. It's been that way since he came out here. Even with everything that happened yesterday, he's still an early riser, and he's been outside sitting in the grass for most of the early morning. By now there's an entire basket of food in front of him.

Unlike most places, the people of Vita are grateful that their government has been toppled. They probably don't give him gifts because they remember him, but because he's the only one out here. Ocher picks through the assortment, nodding as another child comes up and places a bowl of fruit next to him.

They're so appreciative, they must have been truly miserable.

A hand reaches over to grab something out of the basket and Basel drops down beside him. "Where are *my* gifts?"

"Right here. I don't think they're specifically for me."

Basel peers inside the basket, "I guess they want to show their thanks which works out since all the servants who work here took off immediately after we won." He stretches out and faces the sun, "And how do you feel?"

Ocher takes a quick mental inventory of his injuries and finds that unexpectedly enough, he doesn't feel too bad. The medics had patched him up pretty quickly and sent him off. He had followed after everyone else and claimed a space in the tower and was lucky enough to get a bed. After a full night's rest, he's not

completely healed, but there's not even half the pain of yesterday. "Better," he answers.

"What will you do now?"

"I don't know, it depends. Where's Azure?"

Basel shrugs, "Who knows? Probably somewhere giving up on
you."

Ocher looks up in alarm, "What?"

"Relax. He probably won't. Last night, he just seemed like he was
ready to run away from everything. Better hope he feels better
this morning."

"And you don't care that he might disappear?"

"He's not going to run away from *me*. I'll still be able to contact
him. I'm not the one who broke his heart."

Ocher blinks. "I did not."

"You did," Basel disagrees. "But he won't tell you that."

"Is that why he can't make up his mind about what he wants?"

"No, he *definitely* knows what he wants. He can't make up his
mind if he can trust *you* again." That makes sense, as much as he
hates to admit it. "You haven't exactly been trustworthy lately
and you know how hard he guards himself. You have a lot of
making up to do."

"Yeah."

"You could start by being there when he wakes up," Basel says
pointedly. That's true. He stands and Basel reaches out a hand to
stop him. "Be sure this is what you want."

"What do you mean?"

"You left once and you're clearly kind of interested in Dominicus.
You know what it's like being with Azure and what he demands
of you. If you think you're not going to be able to handle that
in the long run, just leave him alone. Don't try to force yourself

back into his life if you're going to decide it's too much and run away again."

Now *he's* annoyed. He's not interested in Dominicus, it was *one time* and he regretted it almost immediately. "Don't tell me what to do."

Basel rolls his eyes, "You getting annoyed won't change that he's still my friend and that you two still bring out the worst in each other."

"I can handle it."

"I mean it, Ocher. I won't handle his shit with you again."

There's something sharp in the way Basel is looking at him that sets him on edge, like he's already planning what to do if he messes up. If Azure talks to him as much as he talks to Savanta, then Basel might know a lot more about him than the other way around. Basel will make him suffer.

"I got it," he mutters.

"Good."

Inside the tower, his feet carry him to the elevator and back to the same room Azure stayed in last time. He pushes the door open quietly and although the sun is shining throughout, Azure sleeps on unbothered.

Ocher steps across the threshold and sits on the edge of the bed, watching him. He's had forever to think about this and he doesn't want to live his life without Azure anymore. A year is a long time for things to come into perspective.

Azure is a liar, manipulative, and has way more power than he or anyone else needs. Azure also demands so much attention from him, but that's not so bad because he craves that same attention back. Maybe they do bring out the worst in each other, but the last time he remembers being happy was when they were together. He can take everything if it means he's the center of Azure's world again.

"What do you want?"

Ocher startles, glancing down. Azure isn't even looking at him. "How did you know it was me?"

"I can always feel you, even when I don't want to." Ocher runs his fingers across smooth olive skin, skimming over his cheeks, and tangling in Azure's long, loose strands. He feels a soft exhale against his wrist. "Don't," is what Azure says, but he doesn't move or push him away.

Ocher moves closer, leaning down to press a kiss to his mouth. When he pulls back, Azure is staring directly at him and he *finally* feels seen again. He leans back in and Azure presses a hand to his chest, stopping him. "Ocher."

He ignores him and shoves his hand away. "Stop fighting me. I want this and you do too. Make us both happy again."

Azure pauses, searching his eyes for any insincerity, but he's unwavering. He knows what he wants. Ocher finds himself abruptly grabbed by the waist and yanked close enough to squeeze tight. "You better make this worth it."

"I will," he promises.

Because in the end, he doesn't want the choices and decisions, or the independence he thought was so important to have. He wants the full weight of Azure's crushing attention on him, now and forever. Nothing else matters.

CHAPTER 23: AZURE

Azure holds himself over Ocher, looking deep into his gray eyes. Part of him wants to pull back, to avoid getting dragged back into this. He loathes the thought of giving Ocher this much power over him again, but another, stronger, part of him is desperate to have Ocher back with him and be complete again.

He can't be sure if Ocher truly loves him and he's not willing to open himself up to sifting through the other boy's emotions either. What he does find in Ocher's eyes is an apology and a willingness to try.

Azure reaches for the hem of his shirt, sliding it up and only breaking eye contact to let Ocher pull it over his head and lock fingers around his neck. He sighs, going back to this really means putting his heart back on the line. He hates the trust he has to give someone by loving them.

Ocher waits for him to make the next move. It's his choice. He's being offered what he wants more than anything right now and all he has to do is take it. Ocher's right, mistakes were made, but they can both be happy again if he chooses, and knowing Ocher needs to be with him to be happy too is the tipping point.

Azure kisses him, pressing them together and he can feel the exhale of relief Ocher makes. It's not like last time. Last time, it meant nothing to him. They both knew that. This time, it's a claim and Ocher knows this as well.

He reaches a hand down, sliding between Ocher's thighs and

the younger male opens his legs easily for him, barely making a sound as he slips fingers inside.

"You're quiet," Azure mumbles, pressing hot, open mouthed kisses along Ocher's neck.

"Yeah, well, you're gentler than usual too."

"That's because you'll whine if I'm not. We've got time."

Ocher reaches up to grab his face and look him in the eye, "I won't."

He laughs in amusement. Ocher must want to be forgiven even more than he thought. Azure presses a chaste kiss to his mouth, "Don't worry about it." He pulls back and Ocher lifts his hips to help him get the rest of his clothes off.

"You too," Ocher's hands go to his boxers and tug until they're both in a similar state of undress.

Azure shifts upwards, guiding his thighs apart, and locks his gaze on Ocher as he slides in, watching the way his cheeks begin to darken. "Are you going to cry this time too?"

"If you keep looking at me, I will."

"Well, I guess you'll have to cry because I'm not looking away," Azure replies, pushing himself all the way in. "Not going to tell me to go slow?"

"You never listened anyway."

Azure leans forward to cup his cheeks, pressing fleeting kisses to his lips, "I missed doing this with you."

"Mm, I know," he murmurs.

Azure moves his hands to grip Ocher's thighs, spreading them to give himself better access. He pulls out to thrust back in shallowly and watches as Ocher shifts from the rough intrusion, but bears with it.

He takes that as an invitation to continue and goes deeper,

increasing his speed when Ocher tightens around him. Ocher reaches up for him and Azure leans into his arms, letting Ocher's quiet groans fill his ears.

"Azure!" He breathes out, squeezing his arms around him.

"I'm here," he murmurs and trails his hand down between them to wrap around Ocher. The shuddering gasp in his ear tells him it's appreciated.

His hand gives a few fast strokes and Ocher spills over his fingers, thighs clenching around his hips. The way Ocher clamps around him pulls him over too and he stills, riding his high and feeling his warmth fill Ocher's insides. Azure pulls out and gathers Ocher to him, listening as his breathing slows.

Azure kisses the soft skin at the back of his neck, Ocher is warm and satisfied in his arms. He loves it. "What are you thinking?" Azure questions, sliding his fingers through damp strands. Ocher is silent and he tenses, discontent rising just that quickly. "We're back to keeping secrets?"

"No!" Ocher answers, turning immediately in his hold. "I'm just thinking Eren and Erina aren't going to be happy."

"So?"

"Nothing." He looks away, "It's not a big deal. They'll just complain a lot and I don't want to have to explain things to them."

Azure is quiet for a moment. He can't understand why Ocher cares what they think. They can always be kicked out, he never has to see them again. "If you don't want to manage their emotions anymore, then stop. You don't have to. Let them feel how they feel." Azure strokes a thumb along his cheek until Ocher looks at him, "Do they really matter so much?"

"No," he admits. "But, they're my friends and you're supposed to care about your friends. Like how Basel cares about you."

Azure shifts, pulling him in closer. "Basel and I are different. We've known each other forever and I actually like him. And

Sara and Savanta. I don't think you like those two that much and you haven't known them long either. Why force yourself to cater to their feelings when you barely know them?"

"I care because they were my friends while I lived and worked with them."

"If you try and please everyone you have some small friendship with, it's only going to cause you stress. Pick the people you choose to keep close more carefully, and preferably ones who know when to back off." Azure lets go of him to slip beneath the covers, kissing his way down Ocher's stomach. "Besides, I'm the only one who matters, right?"

He smiles at the shaky inhalation he feels beneath his lips, "Right." And that's how it should be.

CHAPTER 24: OCHER

As usual, he wakes first and it lets him study the smooth expanse of Azure's darker skin without interruption. Ocher runs his palm across the width of Azure's back, thinking about how he never really got to appreciate his body. Azure was affectionate, but it was usually Azure touching him and not the other way around.

His fingers slide across Azure's shoulders to sweep his messy hair aside and press a kiss to the center of his back. Ocher presses his chest firmly against Azure's back, letting his hands run over the tightness of his stomach and rest there. It feels like Azure has gotten thinner and he hadn't even noticed.

A warm hand covers his own, "Finished feeling me up yet?"

"No."

"Mm, well go on then," Azure encourages with a yawn.

He presses his face into Azure's neck. His words from earlier are still running on repeat in his mind. If Azure's the one that should matter the most to him, then the reverse should be true as well.

"Azure, do you love me?" They're close enough that he feels the way Azure stiffens against him. "Please say you do," Ocher whispers into his skin. "I want you to. Again, if you stopped."

"...How do you know I ever did in the first place?"

He pulls back with a frown before sliding over Azure's body to settle in front of him, staring into his cautious eyes. "You gave me that bangle."

"So?"

"So, you wouldn't do it for no reason. It took you forever to decide to give it to me."

"And then look at what you did," Azure mutters.

"And then you took it back."

"Maybe."

He huffs in frustration. "Can you talk to me for once? Basel has talked to me more in the past twenty four hours than you have in a year." Azure makes a face and Ocher ignores it to scoot forward and intertwine their legs. "Please?"

Azure stares at a spot over his shoulder and the words come out reluctantly. "I was dying. I used too much energy when I took over Haithen and the effects were killing me. I came to find you because I wanted to see you one last time before I died."

Ocher pulls back in shock, "You *what?*"

"The only reason I agreed to come to Vita was because I didn't have much time left and I knew I could probably drag you along with me. I didn't expect everything that happened here."

"You were going to pull me back into your life and then die on me without saying a word?" Azure is silent and that says enough. He shakes his head, the lows Azure will sink to sometimes. If Basel was right about his heart being broken, then making sure he suffered too was probably payback for that. "I shouldn't be surprised."

"I am selfish," Azure agrees.

"Don't sound so okay with it!"

Azure shrugs, "You're the one who wanted to talk. I was content to lay here and let you keep touching me."

"Fine. Then what?"

"And that's why I ended up draining Ciaran. We were all about to die here and I was too weakened to help anyone."

So, rather than tell him the truth, he lied about that too. Azure would never have told him the truth on his own. "You're so frustrating sometimes."

"I know."

"I'm mad at you for not telling me and because you were really just going to die and leave me here alone."

"Makes sense."

"You can't keep secrets like that anymore. You have to be honest with me," Ocher tells him firmly.

Azure wrinkles his nose, "I'll try, but old habits die hard."

"Yeah well," Ocher leans over to kiss him again. "I'm sure you'll try your best."

◆ ◆ ◆

It's a quiet ride back to Haithen. Azure is a warm presence against his side, his hand tightly enclosing his. Azure had wanted to drive one of the trucks, but he had been insistent that they sit together instead and hadn't let him go until Azure agreed. Azure hadn't put up much of a fight.

Ocher's never been so happy to see this place when they pull up in front of the mansion. Sara beams when he steps out, still clinging to Azure's hand, and Savanta rolls her eyes with a shake of her head. She's always disapproved and that probably won't change anytime soon.

Kronos is there, standing on the steps, waiting impatiently. He looks displeased when he realizes they've all survived. Azure abruptly pulls his hand away, ignoring his protests, to follow Kronos inside.

Basel laughs at him and runs along after Azure, "Please don't send me there to help restore order. I'm too young and pretty for the hard work of rebuilding a country!"

Azure shakes his head at Basel's dramatic display. "I think you're good for at least a few months."

"Thank you! I was planning on taking a little vacation to my own tower for a while. I need to get away from you and your drama."

Ocher walks after them into the conference hall where Haithen's advisors have been hastily convened. He foregoes the chair next to Azure for his lap and he's pleased when Azure doesn't push him off. Two days ago, he would have.

Azure hugs him, burying his face in his back until the highest ranking captain has finished his brief about the entire ordeal, ending with the unorganized state of Vita now. They turn to him to see what he has to say, but Azure hasn't paid them the slightest amount of attention the entire time.

Ocher pats his arm, "They're waiting for you."

Azure looks up over his shoulder to face the rest of the room's occupants and meets Kronos's gaze with a patient smile. "Kronos, as you are the top advisor, I would think you could do the most good in helping Vita reorganize itself. You will take the first rotation there, effective immediately."

"What? I can't go there! Who will advise here?"

"There's a table full of people who enjoy telling me what to do. You, your assistant," Azure glances around the table and points at one man who's doing his best to remain unnoticed. "And he will go. Then you can help resettle the immigrants you were so worried about."

"I have a *job* here!"

"And now you will have one there as well. Don't fail. If you can't handle Vita, I'm not sure that I can trust your judgment here either."

"This is ridiculous! My position is too high to be sent away." Kronos glances around the room for support, but no one will look at him. No other advisor wants to go and most of them are probably already planning how they can take over his position. There's no friendship between the advisors, only the thirst for power.

"Meeting adjourned," Azure announces.

They don't agree with his decision, but he went to Vita like they wanted, and now he's back. Ocher thinks they can all tell he doesn't care what they want.

Azure wraps an arm around his waist and drags him towards the common area, "We're home and I think it's about time to downsize."

"Hmm?"

They step into the living area and the moment everyone catches sight of them, Azure turns and pulls him into a possessive kiss. He shoots a smug look to the siblings afterwards and it's terrible, but Ocher's glad that Azure is laying claim to him once again, so he says nothing. He wouldn't dream of pulling away.

"Ocher, he's awful to you!" Erina complains.

Azure can be, but other times, he's not. Besides, sometimes he deserves it. He wraps his arms around Azure. He doesn't have to care if they don't understand.

"Ocher isn't going to deal with your feelings anymore and it's time for you two to go," Azure tells them.

"You can come with us, Ocher. It's not too late," he hears Eren pleading at him.

He *knows* he could return with them if he really wanted, but it's not what he wants most. The past year has taught him that. Not a day went by when he didn't miss Azure, he won't give this up again. He turns a deaf ear to their words.

Happiness is with the person who ruined him for anyone else and he's satisfied with that.

EPILOGUE

Azure's arms are around Ocher's waist, their heads resting together as he sways them side to side. All the others are leaving today. It'll just be the two of them for the foreseeable future. They're both thrilled about that.

Sara bounces around the lawn in a cotton candy pink dress, ready to get started on her trip. Azure had, of course, given her the money, but Sara wasn't willing to let her go alone, so Basel volunteered to go with her after they take a short rest at his tower first.

Eren glowers over at the couple, disappointed with Ocher's decision, but knowing that there's nothing he can do about it. Azure and Ocher are both content to ignore him, he'll be gone soon enough.

Basel nudges him, "Leave it alone. If you keep testing Azure's patience, you might end up locked up. He's done it for less."

"But he's my friend," Eren protests. "I have to care."

Basel glances over at the two of them, "That might be one sided. Seriously, don't worry about him. Azure won't let him out of his sight anytime soon. My offer is still open though. The best way to get over someone is to meet new people and I could use some company escorting a teenage girl with as much energy as Sara around."

Eren looks back to where Azure and Ocher have started kissing again and sighs hopelessly. "That sounds fun, but I can't leave my sister alone."

"I draw the line at two girls and she's strict. Back to the country you go," Basel replies cheerfully.

Savanta clears her throat, "I do have an extra bedroom now and I'm in need of a roommate."

"You're replacing me already!" Sara shouts dramatically, falling into her older sister's arms. "Taking from me the one place I belong!"

"You're taking off the first chance you get," Savanta replies shrewdly.

"True enough," she laughs before running off to break Azure and Ocher apart.

"You're really just going to let her go off without you?" Erina asks.

"I trust Basel to keep her out of trouble and I can't keep holding her back forever. She's too much like Azure." Savanta answers.

"Good at not caring about other people?"

"More like too good at only letting you see what she wants you to see. Sara is very independent. I guess I never realized how much time they spent together when she was younger."

"Yeah," Erina grimaces. "Who wants *his* influence around?"

Savanta smiles at her in amusement, "He's not all bad. You're welcome to come."

Erina glances over at her brother's pleading eyes, "I suppose a change would be nice."

"Great!" Basel says. "So, we're all decided."

Sara joins them with a hand around each boy's wrist. "Now we're all here to say goodbye!"

"Surprised you managed to pry them off each other," Basel comments.

"It was hard." She hugs Savanta, then skips over to loop her arm through Basel's. "See you in a few months!"

Basel waves as she drags him to the truck, "You know my number if you need me to keep my promise!" He shouts to Azure with a pointed look at Ocher.

"I'll keep that in mind."

Eren hugs his sister and nods reluctantly at Ocher before climbing in after them. He's aware enough to know that trying to hug Ocher goodbye would probably end badly for him.

Savanta pulls Azure into a quick hug. "Try not to get involved in anything for a while, yeah?"

"I'll do my best."

She pats Ocher's shoulder, "See you."

Ocher waves as Erina and Savanta head towards the train station, and then Azure is swooping him up and kissing him, and he's laughing into his mouth and he never wants to leave Azure's arms again.

Printed in Great Britain
by Amazon

15330539R00130